MW00911877

abnormal
results

abnormal results

Cancer
changes
everything

kimberly rae

abnormal results
Copyright © 2015 by Kimberly Rae
www.kimberlyrae.com

All rights reserved. No part of this book may be reproduced or transmitted
in any form or by any means, electronic or mechanical, including
photocopying and recording, or by any information storage and retrieval
system, without permission in writing from the author. Unless otherwise
noted, all Scripture verses taken from the Holy Bible, New King James
Version. Copyright © 1982 Thomas Nelson Inc. Used by permission.

Library of Congress Cataloging-in-Publication Data
Rae, Kimberly
Abnormal results/Kimberly Rae - First edition.
Pages 225
Summary: "Teen Victoria Dane needs order. Her three best friends since
kindergarten are her sense of security, but as they age, Victoria fears
losing them. When one of the friends is diagnosed with leukemia, Victoria
has to decide if she will change as life changes, or if she will hide."-
Provided by publisher.
Library of Congress Control Number: 2015909278
ISBN-13: 978-1512320459
ISBN-10: 1512320455
[1. Cancer-Fiction. 2. Teen Cancer-Fiction. 3. Autism-Fiction. 4. Asperger's
Syndrome-Fiction. 5. Self-realization-Fiction. 6. Teen Coming of Age-
Fiction. 7. School Shooting-Fiction. 8. Self-sacrifice-Fiction.] I. Title. II. Title:
Cancer changes everything.

Printed in South Carolina, the United States of America
The characters and events in this book are fictional. Any resemblance to
real people, living or dead, is coincidental.

Dedicated
to MaKenzie and Amy Grant

to those who fight
and those who love
the fighters

Praise for Abnormal Results:

As the parent of autistic child, I am so impressed by how accurately Kimberly Rae portrays the world of autism. I fell in love with the main character Victoria and found myself cheering her on as she coped with the many challenges she encountered through her autistic-like qualities. Everything was so familiar to what our family has encountered. This book opens the door to the world of autism and gives a hopeful glimpse into those hearts of those who struggle with it. Parents of autistic children and others impacted by autism would benefit greatly from reading Abnormal Results. I am certain anyone who reads it would discover as I did that "abnormal" means the Lord is doing something way beyond what we could ever imagine!
- Susan King, author of *Optimism for Autism*

Abnormal Results was a very interesting book to read. I really loved all the random facts!
- Zac, YA reader

I was truly enamored by Abnormal Results, so much so that I read the entire thing in a three-hour sitting. I found it to be witty, interesting, and real, as well as simply a good read! I loved it, and would read it again in a heartbeat.   *- Cassie, YA reader*

Random Fact: Your stomach has to produce a new layer of mucus every 2 weeks or it will digest itself.

You should know that I collect random facts and keep them in a green notebook that must always be placed third from the left on my bookshelf, next to my red notebook on clichés and my blue notebook on metaphors.

I am aware this is abnormal.

CHAPTER ONE

You know that cheesy phrase about having your ducks in a row? My mom is always saying it when we're running out the door, usually late, on our way somewhere.

My dad says it too. "Do we have all our ducks?" he'll ask Mom, which is funny since there are only two of us kids, and I'm fifteen. I don't often get lost on the way from my bedroom to the front door, though the two times I did have made for a great family joke ever since. That was sarcasm in case you missed it.

Alex, my little brother, wanted in on the fun, but he never could figure out where the ducks were. Mom took him to a park once and showed him a family of ducks swimming in a row across a pond, and tried to explain what a metaphor was, but he being only five at the time understood it about as well as I'm understanding why an x plus a y divided by a z somehow turns into a number.

The whole duck thing is important, because when all your ducks are in a row, it means your life is in order. Things are under control. I had no idea how rare a gift that was, all those little ducks staying right where they should be, until cancer knocked one of mine over.

Not a duck though. A dork. One of us four.

I suppose I should explain the whole dork thing. When we were really little, my three best friends and I were waiting in line at Swirly Cone, one of those side-of-the-road ice cream shops. Baby brother Alex, whose full name is Alexander but he hates it, was hanging out with Mom, telling her about his latest genius creation with sidewalk chalk. I saw his eyes suddenly get real big and he tugged on Mom's arm. "Mom, look!" People all down the line turned to see him point at us and yell, "It's four dorks in a row!"

We've been the four dorks ever since: me, Chad, Alecia and Dan. We were thick as thieves, as Dad used to say (he and Mom like to see who can use the most clichés and metaphors), since kindergarten, back when it didn't matter about boys or girls or who had name brand shoes or who could play sports or not. Things have changed over the years. We've changed. But I was sure nothing was big enough to wedge into our friendship. We'd stay the same forever.

I was wrong.

Random Fact: There are more chickens than people in the world.

If they knew that, would they try to take over?

CHAPTER TWO

We go to the graveyard Tuesdays after school, which isn't as creepy as it sounds. There's a pond in the middle of the grounds, with ducks. Even in early January, the temperature never gets low enough to turn the pond to ice, so our ducks stay all winter.

That day I broke off pieces of my sandwich crust that I'd saved from lunch and threw them into the water, still unnerved about our history lesson at school. Mr. Seecord had taught about Columbine. No one said Keith's name out loud in class, but we were all thinking about him. I shivered. "I hate guns," I said, keeping my eyes on the ducks coming for the bread rather than watching Dan eat. Dan chews with his mouth open and if I look at him I gag. "I don't think anyone should have one."

"But gun control wouldn't get rid of all the guns," Chad said, continuing one of the debates we've been sparring over for years. He always picks the opposite argument, even if he doesn't agree. He just likes arguing. "It only keeps the guns out of the hands of the good people. The criminals will still get weapons from the black market, and then where would we be?"

"Shot dead and turned into zombies, I guess." Alecia gathered her long blond curls into a ponytail then pulled a straw from her massive purse and put it into her can of Coke. Apparently swiping an antibacterial wipe over the whole can still didn't make it safe to touch with her lips. She had already sighed twice, a sure sign she was tired of the conversation. If I looked, I'd probably see her roll her eyes, but she was sitting next to Dan so I kept my gaze on the ducks.

Dan talked with his mouth full. "If Mr. Seecord had been carrying a gun when he got ambushed in Afghanistan, he might still have both arms."

"That's different." I pictured our history teacher and shivered again. "Mr. Seecord was in the military. He's trained to—"

"Can we talk about something else?" Alecia did a bouncy turn toward Dan. "Are you going to the game Friday night?"

"Going?" I could hear the grin in Dan's voice. "I'm in it, babe. You'll find me on the court, leading the team with my nothing-but-net shots." He'd started calling Alecia babe, and for some ridiculous reason, she seemed to like it. She giggled and I swallowed my urge to remind Dan he was the shortest guy on the team and would be spending the game on the bench.

"I'll be there to cheer you on, Dan." Chad popped open his can of root beer and took a sip. Alecia took the can from his hand and tried to wipe it down before he snatched it back. "You coming with me, Vicks?"

I threw him a look before I tossed more bread to the ducks. One problem with having the same best friends since K-5 is that the stupid things you came up with when you were knee-high to a grasshopper (another of my dad's sayings) stick around for life. Like Chad calling me Vicks instead of Victoria. I'm not into the name any more than Alex likes being called Alexander. My parents must have been going through a phase when they decided to name their kids after people who pretty much conquered the known world during their lifetimes. If it was a subliminal power-hungry message, they've got to be disappointed, for neither of us kids have proven to be ambitious. Alex doesn't care about much other than Star Wars and Legos. I care about a lot of things, a whole lot, but none of them fit in the category of taking over the world. I avoid taking roll in class if I can help it.

"I need to study."

Chad kicked the bottom of my shoe with his. "Come on, Vicks. Take a break. It's Dan's first game."

"You've got to come," Dan said. His bag of chips was empty so I could look at him now. He grinned. "If it's a big deal for one dork, it's a big deal to all four, right?"

He knew he'd have me there. "Four dorks forever," I said, tossing the last bit of crust and brushing the crumbs off my jeans. "I'll come for your sake, dork."

"Can we stop with the dork thing?" Alecia adjusted a strap on her heeled boots, then pulled a tube of lip gloss out of her bottomless purse and slathered it on thick enough I was sure some would drip off. "We're not babies, and it's not cute anymore. It's just dumb."

I glanced at the guys. Dan lay propped on his elbows next to Alecia's blanket—she'd been bringing one lately to keep from getting her clothes dirty—and he stared at her glossed lips with a crooked smile like he was hypnotized. He'd be no help. Chad was sprawled out on the other side of Alecia, opposite where I sat. He brushed his bangs off his forehead, looked at Alecia and Dan, then grinned at me and crossed his eyes. Chad didn't have hang-ups about people thinking we were childish. He didn't care what people thought. It was my favorite thing about him.

"Looks like these two don't want to be dorks anymore," Chad said. His voice was joking, but his eyes on me were steady. He knew that little phrase would mean a lot more to me than the others. "Maybe we need a new name."

"I don't want a new name." Alecia sighed and shook her head. "Don't you get it? This whole four friends forever deal. It's like we're a clique but the opposite of a cool one. We're in tenth grade now, not first. Don't you ever want to spread out, spend time with other people, have some different friends?"

"We have lots of friends," I objected.

"You know what I mean."

I did but didn't want to admit it. We'd been happy all these years. Why change something that was great? I sent a pleading look to Chad, who held a hand up, palm toward me, like I was a skittish horse and he wanted to keep me from flipping out. I focused on his hand and breathed in and out, while Alecia stood and wiped imaginary dirt off her flowy hippie skirt.

"I'm going to the game Friday," she said, "but with other people. Some of the cheerleaders invited me."

It shouldn't have bothered me. She wanted to hang out with girls who talked about hair and makeup and shoes and a bunch of other things I didn't care about. She highlighted her hair now and put on mascara, and probably didn't want to be seen with me anymore. I realized I had pulled my knees up to my chest and was about to wrap my arms around them and start rocking. Quickly, I slapped my hands down to the ground and forced my body to stay still. "Okay," I said. "I hope you have fun."

And I told myself I meant it.

Random Fact: A crocodile cannot stick out its tongue.

So how does he show annoyance at his siblings? (Or rather its siblings—don't want to be sexist.)

CHAPTER THREE

I haven't been entirely honest with you about the ducks, or my friends, or me for that matter. The truth is I'm not fifteen. I forget sometimes and really think I am, until someone asks why I'm the only one in my class with a driver's license. I'm not supposed to be in the same grade as the other dorks. And I'm not what most people would call normal.

After my first year of kindergarten, some people decided I needed testing. I remember hearing whispered words, technical terms like Autism and Asperger's , but in the end the important people diagnosed that I didn't quite have either. I just really, really liked things to be in order.

My need for structure and routine was labeled as "significant" by the experts, who told my parents first grade would be too much for me and I'd be better off going through kindergarten a second time. Who fails kindergarten? They said I was "developmentally challenged" and it would help me to learn how to adapt to free play and other things that were hard for me because they weren't structured. I don't remember having a hard time during free play, but it seems the experts did not think that my arranging all the blocks in perfect lines according to color and shape was healthy.

I need things to be in order. Like ducks in a row. We joke in our family about mom always asking that when we leave the house, but I know it is our secret code, just between her and me. She's asking if everything is in order. If I'm okay, and things are as they should be, so we can leave the house without me...I don't know, panicking I guess. She says when I was little if I was putting my toys in perfect rows and we had to leave the house before I'd finished, I would start screaming.

I don't scream when things aren't orderly anymore. Not on the outside anyway. That's almost entirely due to Mom's unending patience, and my friends, the dorks. That second year in kindergarten, Chad and Dan and Alecia befriended me and stuck with me that entire year. They showed me how to play with the other kids instead of sitting at my desk arranging pencils through recess. They taught me how to act normal enough that I didn't scare my classmates away.

Chad would practice phrases with me for hours, having me repeat them with the right intonation so I would sound warm and friendly.

"Good morning. How are you?"

"I'm fine. How are you?"

"See you later."

"Have a nice day."

Dan taught me to throw and catch a ball. And his laugh was so contagious, I learned to laugh just from being around him.

Alecia brushed and braided my hair, kept my shoes tied, and kept me close to her when other girls came around. She knew how to talk and make friends, and when I was with her, people accepted me.

With them, I was safe. The dorks didn't care that I was a year behind. Over time I stopped caring too. I wanted it to stay that way forever.

Thinking of things changing makes me scream on the inside.

Random Fact: There are two words in the English language that have all five vowels in order: "abstemious" and "facetious."

As I have never encountered the word "abstemious" in my entire life, I don't think it should count.

CHAPTER FOUR

"Chad, we have to find a way to stop Alecia," I said, my rear already sore from sitting on the bleachers through the first half of Dan's game. I would need to either gain ten pounds or get a cushion if they made it to the championships. "You have to think of something."

"I don't think this is a problem to fix, Vicks," Chad said. "If Alecia needs more friends or different friends, we shouldn't stand in her way."

"But we promised to be friends forever." I tried very hard to not sound like a whiny kid.

"Friendships change over time. You know that." Chad craned his neck to see Dan on the bench. He hadn't played a second yet, but he still looked unreasonably happy. His bench couldn't be as hard as the one I was sitting on.

Our high school is small as far as public schools go. Its claim to fame used to be the yearly hot dog eating contest the town had on the football field every summer, which is not much of a claim and didn't earn much fame. Keith Childers changed all that. Last March, when we were freshmen, Keith was the reason our school made every major news channel in the country. They didn't even have the hot dog eating contest last year. The whole town was what my kindergarten psychiatrist would diagnose as traumatized. I remember asking Mom how they would have survived if he'd done what he threatened to do, and she said that fear paralyzed people, even if what they feared never came to pass.

I saw her words play out as metal detectors appeared one morning in our hallways and security guards were hired to wander around the grounds, trying to look unobtrusive, which was impossible. Eventually the hassle of students being late because their watches and necklaces and cell phones kept making the metal detectors go off was too much for somebody high up in the school board, so they got removed. I asked Mrs. Slessor, our homeroom teacher, what happened to them, but she didn't know. Did they get donated to some poor school where students weren't allowed to wear watches? Did the principal sell them on eBay?

"What happened to the guards?" I shifted to look behind the bleachers in case they were patrolling back there, but couldn't see even one. "I hadn't thought about it till now, but I haven't seen any since we got back from Christmas break."

It was nice, being in tenth grade. Last year, high school was a new place with new routines and a bigger student body than middle school. I spent a lot of evenings last year in my bathtub.

If you're thinking I don't sound like a sixteen-year-old, it's okay. People who aren't the dorks have told me I sound like I'm thirteen, or maybe fourteen on a good day. I tell them I'm developmentally challenged, so it could be worse, and then I freak them out by crossing my eyes and quoting *Green Eggs and Ham* by Dr. Seuss. They start looking around, hoping no one they know is watching them interact with me, and then come up with some excuse to leave quick. So you're free to think I sound younger than a normal sixteen-year-old, but you might not want to say it to my face.

"Didn't you hear?" Chad asked. He chugged down his can of Mountain Dew. I've told him a million times that sugary drinks are bad for his teeth, not to mention his brain, but he ignores me. "It was a big argument over the break. The school board said the guards were costing the school too much money. The principal and the teachers wanted to keep them."

Some player ran the ball down the court and made a three-pointer, and I had to wait for everyone to stop cheering before we could talk again. Funny how my screaming as a kid was considered inappropriate behavior, but in other settings, people yell like barbarians and everyone calls it fun. When we were kids, I would crouch down and cover my ears with my hands when the noise got loud at games like this. Alecia got so embarrassed she refused to sit with me anymore unless I stopped. Dan rescued me by putting his hands over my ears like it was a joke, but he held on so hard I had to remain standing. Eventually, he let go one finger at a time until I could stay upright without him. I still get the shakes inside, especially when I'm not paying attention and the screaming surprises me, but I hold my breath and sing "four little ducks went out to play" in my head until things calm down.

The people around us finally settled and I turned to Chad. "So I'm guessing the school board won."

Chad nodded, his eyes on the game. He got all jittery when our team was winning, and he was dangerously close to sloshing his drink all over his pants. It had happened before. "In the end, they said since Keith was in a juvenile detention center, we were safe, and the guards were a constant reminder to the students of what might have happened, so they should go."

I felt the corners of my mouth turn up. "Bet they got all the parents on that one."

"Yep." Some girls walked by and a few waved up at Chad. He'd filled out over the past year and his face had lost its little boy look, and now he was getting attention from girls. They'd giggle and toss their hair and act like idiots trying to get him to notice. If he didn't notice, which he often didn't because his mind was on the game, or the teacher in class, or an actual conversation, they'd send dagger looks my way. I have to admit feeling a strong sense of satisfaction during those moments. All the face paint in the world can't compete with having something interesting to say. Or just being able to sit with a friend without expecting anything. Those girls expected a lot.

"What do you think about flirting?" I blurted out, wishing I could take the words back the moment they left my mouth. Aside from that one moment in eighth grade, Chad and I always acted like brother and sister. I didn't want him to think I had a crush on him or anything.

"In general or specifically?" Chad was grinning, but he still didn't look my way, which was good since my face was burning and probably looked all red and blotchy.

"In general," I said quickly, gesturing toward the gaggle of girls at the base of the bleachers. "It seems since we started high school, it's the thing to do."

He shrugged. "I'm not into it. Flirting seems to me what guys and girls do when they don't have anything in common to actually talk about."

I wished that girl who kept glancing up at Chad could hear him. My face cooled until he added with a smile, "But if you're also asking specifically, like, say, because you want to learn to flirt with my brother..."

My cheeks were on fire again and I choked on my drink of water. I put the bottle down and coughed. "Not funny," I said.

He laughed when I turned away, crossed my arms, and acted like I was suddenly interested in the game. "Hey, they put Dan in. What a shocker."

Chad nudged me with his shoulder. "You don't fool me, Vicks," he said, still laughing. He reached in front of me so I could see when he pointed several rows down the bleachers.

"Cameron is sitting over there. Don't tell me you didn't notice."

"I didn't." And it was true. At least I hadn't until Chad pointed him out. I told myself to keep it that way. *Don't notice him. Don't notice.*

For the rest of the game, Chad's older brother might as well have been coated in neon paint.

Random Fact: All 50 states are listed across the top of the Lincoln Memorial on the back of the $5 bill.

Pardon me while I go check that out.

CHAPTER FIVE

Some people like to take bubble baths to relax. I like to sit in an empty bathtub, fully clothed, with the curtain closed. It's where I hide. Where I can put my thoughts in order.

That's where Mom found me the morning after the game. I was still in my pjs, but she didn't scold. It was Saturday and I had checked the calendar the night before. January ninth was blank. I like blank days. They mean I can take as long as I want to get ready in the morning. I get to arrange my clothes and my socks and my shoes, which degenerate into chaos throughout a week of rushing to get to school on time.

"You okay?" Mom asked. She drew the curtain to the side and sat on the edge of the tub, but kept a few inches away. I didn't mind being touched like I used to, but I still didn't like to be surprised by it. She always gave fair warning if a hug or something was coming. If I knew, I could tell myself to enjoy it, and often I did. When I was in the bathtub, though, she knew I was upset, and that's never a good time for touching. They tell me that with most people, it's the opposite, but I have a hard time believing it.

"I'm okay," I said, resting my cheek against my knees and tapping my bare toes on the porcelain veneer of the tub floor. "Things are changing. I have to change. That is hard."

Mom smiled. I loved how she never acted like she minded me being me. She reached across and touched one of the four rubber duckies lined in a perfect row on the windowsill to my left. Why anyone would put a window on a wall next to a bathtub was a mystery to me. Who wanted to look outside while taking a bath? I kept the blinds down over that window. Only a few lines of light filtered through to land on my ducks.

"Remember when I first got these for you?" she asked, picking up one of the ducks and turning it over to see Alecia's name printed on the bottom. "You were seven years old. I bought them to help you enjoy bath time, but when I put them in the water, you hated how you couldn't get them to stay together in a line."

"Like the ducks in the pond."

She laughed softly. "You took them out of the water, named them, and put them on the windowsill so—and I quote—they could 'stay in a row like they're supposed to.'"

I felt myself rocking slightly back and forth. "That one," I said, gesturing to the duck in Mom's hand, "wants to leave the line."

Mom set Alecia's duck back in its place, and after her hand moved I nudged the duck until it was positioned at the correct angle to match the others. "She does?" Mom asked. I also liked how she never acted surprised or too dramatic about things. It helped.

"She thinks us being the four dorks is..."

Mom smiled. "Dorky?"

She could always make me smile too. "Yeah."

"Well, that's reasonable, considering dork is an archaic word used by old folks like me and your dad." She reached a hand out, very slowly, and put it on my knee. "Alecia wants different things right now than you do, Victoria, and that's okay. People don't have to be the same to stay friends."

"But the friendship changes." Part of me wanted to pick up my ducks and hold them, but the part of me that wanted them to stay perfectly aligned kept my hands around my legs.

"Yes, you're right." Mom took her hand from my knee and used it to grab a towel bar on the wall and pull herself up to a standing position. "You'll find throughout your life that friendships change. Some will stay. Some will go. Some will be more or less than they were."

"But doesn't it mean something bad if someone used to want to be my friend and now they don't?"

"Not necessarily." Mom arranged the towel she had mussed. She liked order too, just not quite as much as I did. She turned and looked at me. "If Alecia wanted other friends because you were unkind to her or you started to be selfish, that would be bad. If it's just because you have different interests, that's not bad at all. You wouldn't want her to expect you to fake being like her to keep her friendship, would you?"

I imagined trying to giggle, or curling my hair and going shopping for hours on end. My nose wrinkled up. "No."

Mom smiled. "Then don't expect it of her."

She left and I stared at Alecia's duck. There wasn't anything wrong with the things Alecia cared about now. It was important to be true to who you were. Therefore—

The door opened and Mom's head popped back into view. "Has Chad talked to you?"

Her tone was different. "He talks to me every day. What do you mean?"

The space between her eyebrows scrunched. She did that when she was worried about something. "I was just wondering. His mom told me they had an important doctor's appointment this week, and I..." She trailed off and then did her forced smile. "Well, I just wondered if you'd heard anything."

She disappeared again and left me wondering what "important" meant when referring to a doctor's appointment. And who were "they"? Chad hadn't said anything about an important appointment, or any appointment at all.

I told myself to take the ducks off the windowsill, or at least move them so they weren't in order. I needed to accept that friendships change.

I touched the ducks. Pushed them slightly out of sync.

I couldn't do it. Carefully, I put each back until they were all where they should be.

Random Fact: An ostrich's eye is bigger than its brain.

Is that worse than your eyes being bigger than your stomach?

CHAPTER SIX

Our history teacher scares me. Mr. Seecord's not a scary guy. Some kids are intimidated by his missing arm, but I'm not. I find that fascinating—though I don't tell people anymore. I told the dorks once and Dan said I was weird and Alecia said I was gross. I don't mean it in a gross way. I'd like to ask him how it has changed his life. How does he brush his teeth? How does he get his shirt on?

But I'll never ask. Not about his arm. And not about Keith Childers and his guns, though I've wanted to for almost a year.

What scares me about Mr. Seecord is thinking about how he lost his arm, about weapons and war and violence. To think of people hating other people so much they would kill makes me want to go hide in the bathtub and never come out.

So today in class, when Mr. Seecord quoted whatzisface's famous statement, "Give me liberty or give me death," I had to grab my desk with both hands to keep from running out of the room.

"I have a special assignment for you today," he said. Lexie Thomas, up in the front row, sat up and beamed. She loved special assignments. Dan, two rows behind me, groaned. No need to say how he felt about them.

"Get out your homework notebooks and write this down." Mr. Seecord grabbed a new piece of chalk and wrote on the board, *What is worth dying for?* He turned to face us. I hoped he would not notice I had not written down the assignment. I was still holding on to my desk. "You may agree with Patrick Henry that liberty is worth dying for, or you may not. My question to you isn't about liberty, but about life. What do you believe is worth living for?"

Billy Sanders raised his hand. "Didn't you say worth dying for?"

"Ah, but that's the point." Mr. Seecord nodded, his wizened eyes glancing over our clueless faces. He wasn't old. His hair was dark brown and cut short, like he was still in the Marines. His face was tan and his build was lean but strong. When he talked about war in history class, any war, we listened. Sometimes, not often, he would forget he was talking to us. His gaze would wander out the window, as if he could see all the way to Afghanistan, and his voice would drop low and he'd talk about his year there. We would go still and silent, no one wanting to drop a pencil or shift a desk and remind him he was a high school teacher now with students hanging on his every word. Once, he talked about the day he lost his arm. It was after a raid. He had set his gun down to help a wounded guy, an Afghani, get on his feet when the second attack came. As he dragged the wounded man toward cover, a missile exploded in the ditch he was going to hide in. The delay caused by helping a fallen stranger saved his life.

Alecia had started crying and he realized where he was. He apologized. The guys begged him to finish the story, but he walked back to his desk and continued his lesson on the Civil War right where he'd left it. I saw the sheen on his forehead though, and knew that day was still on his mind. I wondered if he would be better off teaching math, or science, or some other subject that wasn't about this and that war. To us wars were words in bold on the page we had to memorize for a test. Who won. How many died. To him they were memories.

"Victoria?"

I jerked upright. "Yes, sir?"

"Write the assignment." Mr. Seecord's mouth quirked into his half smile and Alecia sighed like a fan girl. "And pay attention, please."

I pried one hand from my desk and told it to write the assignment and keep my eyes on the paper so I wouldn't notice if everybody was looking at me or not. I shouldn't have gotten lost in thought. I work hard at avoiding any reason to draw attention to myself, by the teacher or the students.

"As I was saying." Mr. Seecord paced around the room as he talked. Marched might be a better word. "If we can decipher what we believe is worth dying for, we often discover what is worth living for. I'd like you to keep that in mind as you write this essay. It can be as long or as short as you'd like, but you have to answer the question to your own satisfaction."

Lance Cade, who wore the trendiest, most up to the minute fads in a futile attempt to be cool, smirked. "Can we just write no?"

Mr. Seecord didn't laugh. It was nice that he didn't act all buddy-buddy with students. "Would that answer satisfy you?" he asked Lance.

"I guess not," Lance mumbled. I smiled. Mr. Seecord had once said that respect and admiration were things to be earned, and no one could buy or bully their way into anyone's heart. I'd written that on a card right away.

I collect phrases like that—words put in order so they are powerful and have deep meaning. I like clichés and metaphors too, but they go in their designated notebooks. I put powerful quotes on index cards in labeled boxes in my room. My favorite from Mr. Seecord is, "The right choice isn't always the safe one."

"Does anyone have any ideas to get started?" he asked. A few hands went up. Not mine; they were back to keeping a grip on my desk.

"Family," one student offered.

"Faith," added another.

One kid who thought he was funny said, "Pizza," which got a sort of laugh from a few students until they saw Mr. Seecord's face. He wasn't just unimpressed. He was angry.

"If you had friends die for what they believed in, you wouldn't take this question lightly."

Total silence. We stared at his face as he wiped at his eyes with the back of his hand, then turned away from us. The bell rang and we filed out of the classroom without a word. As I did every time, I thought of the question I wanted to ask him, but I wouldn't have then even if I'd had the courage.

"Do you know the answer?" Chad asked once we were in the hallway.

"To the essay question?" I shifted to better balance my heavy backpack between my shoulders. Why did books have to weigh so much?

"Uh huh." He looked back into the room. Mr. Seecord was at the window, looking out. "He decided freedom was worth dying for, and I really respect that." Chad looked at me then. "I don't know if I feel that way. I don't know if there's anything I would be willing to die for."

I thought of my family, of my four ducks in a row. Some people would say God or country. It was easy to come up with a word in theory, but he said the answer had to satisfy us, not a criteria for a grade. "I don't know either."

We walked to our next class together. "I guess it's a good thing he gave us till the end of the quarter." Chad waved at friends along the way, people I didn't even notice.

"Yeah," I said, though inside I did not agree. That meant weeks of thinking about living and dying. I did not like thinking about death. It was not something you could control or keep in order, so it did not belong in my world.

Random Fact: Babies are born without kneecaps. They don't appear until the child reaches 2 to 6 years of age.

Now I really want to find a baby and touch its knees. Are they squishy?

CHAPTER SEVEN

Alecia and Dan weren't in Mr. Seecord's history class and thus did not need to figure out about life and death. When we gathered around a pizza in Chad's basement that Friday, a tradition started once when we all had to cram for a test on fractions, they instead talked about the essay Mrs. Wagner assigned them.

"You're supposed to explain why the Berlin Wall came down? That's it?" I flopped a piece of pepperoni and mushroom from the box onto a paper plate and then dropped onto one of Chad's super mushy bean bag chairs. "We're supposed to decide what's worth dying for and you get to spout facts on paper?"

Chad piled three pieces of pizza onto his plate and sat on an old ratty eggplant-purple couch his parents had bought at a thrift store back when they were just starting out and poor as dirt. They'd tried to sell it at every yard sale they'd had as long as I could remember, but nobody else wanted it. Chad loved it and said he was going to buy it himself and put it in the center of his living room someday. I warned him doing so might result in lifelong singleness. "Would you rather be doing their report than ours?" he asked me.

I pondered while I chewed that first amazing bite of extra cheese. "I guess not," I admitted. As much as I did not like the topic, I was a sucker for a challenge. "But with theirs I could throw in a lot of big words."

Dan had been sort of cooing at Alecia in a gross way over the pizza box. He turned to look at me. "You can't talk fancy in your report?" It was a well-known fact by the dorks that, as a voracious reader, my vocabulary was advanced for my age. Unfortunately, all the big words I learned were just in letter form and I often mispronounced them, which caused that kind of laughter I avoid, so these days I try to only use them in writing or around other kids who don't know what the words mean anyway so they don't know when I butcher the pronunciation.

"He wants sincerity and personal belief."

Alecia tore off half a piece of Dan's second slice of pizza and nibbled at it like a hamster. On a diet. "Since we have different reports, maybe Dan and I should go work on ours over there." She pointed with her pizza to a corner away from us.

Chad shook his head and I inwardly cheered. "We've got all quarter to work on the reports. Tell us about your ball game coming up, Dan."

Dan was at Chad's side in less than ten seconds. Alecia let out her trademark sigh for the day and settled next to me in the second bean bag.

While Dan regaled us with basketball statistics and the new plays that were sure to get them to the championships this year—according to him—I took the time to study my friends.

Most of the time, I didn't think about what they looked like or what they wore. They were staples in my life, like cereal for breakfast or feeding the ducks at the pond on Tuesdays. We'd all grown taller and developed our individual styles—though mine would be more a lack of style—but it happened so gradually, day by day, it didn't feel like we were changing.

Dan was the jock of our quartet. His shoulders were wide, and him being short made them look even wider. His nose was slightly crooked and people assumed he'd broken it, but it had just grown that way naturally. He had a big grin and floppy blond hair and was never more excited than when someone brought up sports. I think Alecia was determined to change that, but as was clear from his choice to talk basketball with Chad over study time with her, it hadn't happened yet.

My gaze slid over to Chad, who was by definition, according to several girls at school, dreamy. He had olive skin and dark hair that curled just at the edges, and all his features were asymmetrical, which according to studies makes the face more attractive to the human eye. He had the kind of looks that got his picture in the yearbook more than most, got him invited to those annoying events where the girl has to ask the guy, and would probably land him a role as heartthrob teen in a movie if he ever felt inclined to be an actor. It got to him, the attention he got, but not in a big head way. He thought being liked just for his looks was shallow and I agreed. There were a hundred more reasons to like Chad, but most people never got past staring at his face to find them.

Me, I didn't have that problem. Nobody stared at my face. It wasn't a bad face. Just normal. My looks are the one thing about me that fits into the ordinary category. Average height, average build, sandy brown hair that's not quite wavy but not quite straight. If I had ugly friends, I might look better, but hanging around Alecia is like standing next to a star. I get lost in the glow, and that's just fine with me.

I didn't like thinking about my own looks because it reminded me I'd forgotten to brush my hair after school, a necessary evil on cold, wet days like this. I probably looked like I'd rubbed a balloon on the carpet then on my head like Alex was fond of doing to me lately. I ran my fingers through the tangles and turned my attention to Miss Glow beside me.

Alecia was a classic beauty. Her long, wavy hair did what she wanted it to do, thanks to a collection of bottled products and a somewhat serious investment of time in my opinion. She had a willowy shape and long legs, which went great with her new penchant for bohemian skirts and calf-high boots. She had taken the boots off and propped her feet up on the couch near where Dan sat. Her toenails were painted cherry red and her nails were a lighter shade of the same hue. So was her lip gloss, now that I thought about it. Did she always make them all coordinate like that?

"Why are you staring at me?" she whispered sideways. She had great peripheral vision. Peripheral was one of the words I never pronounced right.

"I'm admiring your talent at utilizing the color red."

She used a finger to lift her necklace from her sternum, which also fit her color scheme. (I refer to her necklace being red, not her sternum, just to clarify.) "I have one just like it in sea foam green." She glanced at me. "People don't normally talk that way, you know."

"What way?"

She rolled her eyes. "Utilize the color red. Why don't you just say, cool necklace? Or, I like your toenail polish?"

"Cool necklace," I tried. "And I like your toenail polish."

That made her laugh, which felt good. "We should go shopping sometime, Vicky." She saw the look of mild terror on my face and interjected quickly, "Not a big long spree. Just long enough to get you one decent outfit. And matching accessories."

I was about to say something about using my money to save a whale or a sea lion when Chad's mom came downstairs. This was a rare event. She hated the eggplant couch and whenever she saw it, inevitably a yard sale loomed on the horizon, so she mostly stayed upstairs. The fact that I could count at least seven of Chad's socks in random places around the room might also contribute to her avoidance.

We all sat up a little, like teens do when an adult suddenly appears. Even if you aren't doing anything wrong, you still feel in trouble, like when you drive by a policemen and slow down, even if you were doing twenty-five. She didn't notice. It was odd, usually she had lots of nice things to say or interesting questions to ask. Today she looked like she'd been crying.

I noticed Chad did not look at her. He kept his eyes on his pizza. "What's the word, Mom?" he asked.

She stopped at the foot of the stairs. Her eyes were red. She had definitely been crying. Alecia asked, "Are you okay, Mrs. Carlson?"

She looked from Chad to Dan to Alecia and finally to me. "We've been called back to the hospital. They need to do more tests."

Like puppets pulled by invisible strings, we all stood. I packed up the leftover pizza and put the used napkins in the empty box. I think we were all afraid to ask what Mrs. Carlson's sickness was. It must be bad. She was obviously upset. "You should go to the hospital with her," I whispered to Chad as I looked for the trash can. It was in a different place every time I came over. Another one of those tricks Chad liked to play to keep me from getting into an orderly rut. Personally, I think he just enjoyed messing with my mind.

"Yeah, I'm going with her," Chad said. His eyes were dark.

Alecia put her hand on Mrs. Carlson's arm. A normal gesture. I wished I had thought of it. "I'm sorry," she said.

"We don't know anything for sure. Not yet." She wiped her eyes. "Chad, we need to go."

He nodded. "You guys can hang out here if you want. Alecia, looks like you'll get to work on your report after all."

She smiled and rubbed his arm a little. "Just until you get back."

"He probably won't be back tonight," Mrs. Carlson said. She started crying again and turned to go back up the stairs. "I'll get some things ready."

I did not touch him, but I did come to stand close. "Chad?"

He looked at me and a muscle in his jaw jerked. "It's probably nothing. I don't want to talk about it."

Random Fact: Peanuts are one of the ingredients of dynamite.

That is so random, I can't even think of anything to say about it.

CHAPTER EIGHT

We were watching a movie about Alexander the Great the next afternoon, an old one from the sixties or seventies because ever since Disney botched up *Pocahontas*, my mother didn't trust Hollywood's modern take on anything that had to do with history.

I wasn't sure if Mom thought *Alexander the Great* would inspire Alex to greatness, or she just liked the story. I found it rather depressing. This guy with extra doses of ambition and self-promotion goes on to take over the world and finds the success empty in the end. At least that's how it ends if they finished the movie according to history. I didn't make it that far.

Alex bemoaned the fact that the guys were wearing miniskirts and Mom was explaining about Roman fashion when the phone rang. Mom and Dad both use cell phones instead of a land line, and she keeps hers in her pocket, so the ring startled all three of us on the couch. She paused the movie and answered. I still can picture that scene on the TV, men and horses frozen in time, waiting to go into battle.

"Are you sure?"

Silence.

"I don't—I don't know what to say."

Mother always knew what to say. I sat up, recognizing Mrs. Carlson's voice through the phone. "Is she still in the hospital?" I whispered to Mom.

Mom put a hand up to shush me. "I'm so sorry, Gloria. So very sorry. What can we do?"

More murmuring from the phone.

"I'll tell her. She's here right now."

I hadn't been able to understand Mrs. Carlson's words through the phone, but I could tell she was crying now. They must have diagnosed her with something terrible.

"We'll come right over," Mom said. She closed the call and looked out the window and breathed in and out twice. She wasn't aware of it, but she always did that before saying something she didn't want to say. It was always two breaths, never just one.

"Can we turn the movie back on now?" Alex asked. He loved movies that had to do with war, even if the guys were in miniskirts.

Mom picked up the remote but used it to turn the TV off.

"Aw, I want to watch the end," Alex whined.

Mom turned to me and tears were in her eyes. I got this tight, clenched-up feeling in my chest that what she had to say would change my life somehow.

"Victoria," she said. "Chad has cancer."

Not-So-Random Fact: The word cancer is related to the Greek word crab because its finger-like projections are similar to the shape of the crab.

I'm picturing those fingers reaching all through Chad's body. Today is a terrible day.

CHAPTER NINE

Whoever came up with the cancer word should have made it bigger. It should take up more space in your mouth when you say it and on a page when you write it, because it takes up so much space in life whenever it appears. Already I felt it sucking up the air around me. It was almost tangible, the way it spread and filled the spaces in our house, and then the car as Mom drove me to Chad's house. He wasn't there; he was still in the hospital, but both the Carlson cars were at the hospital too, and Chad's mom asked us to bring Cameron. Alex stayed home with dad to watch the rest of the movie. Mom wasn't sure if they'd let little kids into Chad's room. She didn't say it, but I knew she didn't want him catching something.

"Cancer isn't contagious, Mom," I pointed out as we rode.

"I know that, Victoria." Her voice was tense. She'd been holding back tears the entire eight minutes since the phone call. "But there are a lot of people in the hospital with sicknesses other than cancer. It's flu season, and people get pneumonia in the winter, and—"

She continued but I stopped listening. We pulled into Chad's drive and even the house looked different. It wasn't different, but it felt like it was. Cancer lived there now, or would once Chad came home.

We found Cameron in the basement. It was a wreck and so was he. His eyes looked hollowed out and I wondered if he'd gotten any sleep the night before. He'd known the testing was for Chad, and now he knew his little brother had cancer. I tried to imagine how that would feel but even thinking about it hurt too much.

He stood and Mom hugged him and then asked a bunch of questions and kept her hand on his arm like any reassuring friend—except me—would do. What did I do? I picked up Chad's discarded socks and put them in a pile on the steps to take up and put in the laundry. I moved the trash can to an easy spot to access and found a few more napkins to throw away. I cleaned up Cameron's empty candy bar wrappers and hunted lint stuck between the cushions of the couch. When I ran out of things to put in order I stood and waited for Mom or Cameron to say something or do something that would make sense of the world.

They didn't. "Let's go," was all Mom said.

We rode in silence: Mom, Cameron, me, and the word none of us would say, which was why there was nothing to say.

I don't know much about cancer. It's not the kind of thing you learn about unless you have to. I know it kills people, and if it doesn't kill them, there's always the chance that it will come back. So the ones who survive live with this cancer cloud hanging over them for life.

We arrived and as soon as we got into the lobby, the three of us were absorbed into different groups of anxious people. Mom got flanked by Chad's parents, particularly his mom, who needed a shoulder to cry on and a new box of Kleenex. The box in her hand was empty and the wad of tissues in her other hand looked soggy already. Cameron's friends made a huddle around him. I recognized one or two of them but most were strangers.

I expected to sit alone in my mental cancer wasteland, but Alecia and Dan stood up from chairs at the opposite side of the room and came my way. Mrs. Carlson must have called them. I had not thought of that. I had not thought of much of anything. That word filled my head like a balloon.

Alecia hugged me and asked a pile of questions that I didn't have answers to. Dan stood still next to me, like he used to when a bee flew around his head and he was scared to move. He was terrified of bees. I guess he was terrified of cancer too. Like the rest of us.

"What are we going to do?" Alecia's voice was small and young. I noticed her hair was damp at the roots and wondered if she'd been drying it when she got the call. Would she remember that moment forever, the way my parents talk about what they were doing when the Twin Towers fell, or my grandparents when JFK got shot? People just living life when, bam, everything flips over on you.

"I don't know." The disorder in the waiting room bothered me. Not the magazines lying around or the random pieces of trash left on a seat here or there. It was the people. The way they hovered and talked but couldn't seem to find a place to land. The anxiety in the room was like an elephant moving around. Everybody kept ducking but it still kept smashing into people and squeezing the life out of them.

So they'd get up and wander to another seat, or go get a drink, or pace. The elephant would follow though. There was no getting away.

A doctor appeared and the adults converged on him like cult followers do their leader. He led Chad's parents to a set of vacant chairs. They waved Cameron over and the rest of us came uninvited. We surrounded the man in the white coat and listened to words about platelets and bone scans and white blood cells. We stared blankly until he got to the part about the results being abnormal. I felt the air stiffen around me along with the people.

"I'm very sorry," the doctor told Mr. and Mrs. Carlson. "Your son has leukemia."

Alecia started crying. I backed out of the group while the doctor reassured everybody with the latest success stories. Mom caught up with me on the way out the door. "Victoria, are you okay?"

I shook my head no and kept walking. She drove us home. I went upstairs without a word to anyone. I needed to research leukemia on the internet. Find out everything I could. Print out pages of herbal remedies or modern cocktail drug options. Arm myself with information and an arsenal of helpful advice.

Instead, I went straight up to the bathroom and spent the evening rocking in a tub, Chad's rubber duck clutched tight in my hand.

Random Fact: Three hundred million cells die in the human body every minute.

Why couldn't the dying ones be the cancer ones?

CHAPTER TEN

"I'm a lousy friend."

Chad opened his eyes just a slit and half-smiled. "Hey," he said.

"Hey." I made my way through the maze of medical equipment and stood by his bed. "I'm sorry."

"That I have cancer or that you ran away last night without saying hi?"

"Yes."

His smile twitched. "Dan and Alecia stayed till visiting hours were over."

"I'm a coward."

"Yes, you are."

His eyes closed, like it was too much effort to hold his eyelids up. I took a look around the room and ended back at him again. "You look pretty miserable."

"Thanks for noticing. I feel pretty miserable too."

"I'm sorry."

He grimaced. "I've heard that a lot the last twenty-four hours."

I did not know how to respond. This was the point where normal people would ask questions. What were platelets? What was his white blood cell count? What medicine did they have him on and did they think it would work? Would he have to do chemo or radiation? In other words, most people came

42

up with words to fill in the gaping hole left by the only question that mattered but nobody wanted to ask.

Are you going to die?

"Well?"

I snapped to attention. "What?"

"Are you going to pull up a chair and sit with me, or do you want to run away again?"

"I want to run away," I said honestly, reaching for a chair against the wall and sliding it next to his bed. "But I'm going to stay."

"Good for you." He put his hand out and tweaked the chair slightly off center. Old habits die hard. I put it back. Like I said...

He chuckled and put his hand on the guard rail of the bed. I guessed he must be in danger of rolling off because they were up on both sides. He pushed a button and a voice came through. "Could I have some water, please?" Chad asked the voice.

"Be right there," it responded.

"So you get room service here," I said. "Nice."

"Yep, all the free water I want." He had lifted his head to talk but dropped it back onto his pillow. "Whatever you do, don't say there's a reason for this, and don't tell me about some herbal cure you found on the internet last night."

"Wouldn't dream of it. I was going to hold your hand and weep all over your arm until your skin shriveled up like you'd been in the bath for an hour."

"That sounds fun." A nurse came in and held a cup of water with a kiddy straw bent so Chad could drink without sitting up.

"You know, you're a lousy friend too," I said when she left.

"Yeah? How's that?"

I thought of all the ways he was a wonderful friend and was in danger of actually weeping on his arm. "Why didn't you tell us that something was wrong? What kind of guy doesn't tell his best friends he's sick?"

"The kind that hoped it would go away. Or not be anything important." Chad sighed. "It wasn't like there was a big oh-no-maybe-I-have-cancer moment. I just started feeling like crud and then I got a cut that wouldn't heal and they said there was a problem with my blood not clotting, and next thing you know here I am, getting x-rays and a spinal tap and everybody's talking about my platelet count."

"Which is...?"

He pulled a folded sheet of paper off the bedside table and handed it to me. "I got tired of saying it over and over again."

I unfolded the printout and read aloud. "Leukemia is a type of cancer found in your blood and bone marrow and is caused by the rapid production of abnormal white blood cells. These abnormal white blood cells are not able to fight infection and impair the ability of the bone marrow to produce red blood cells and platelets."

It went on to big words like "lymphocytic" and "myelogenous" and then got so technical I stopped reading and skimmed down to a section I could understand, about how decades of research vastly improved the outcome for kids with a certain type of leukemia. Was Chad still considered a child in this case? Did he have that certain kind? I didn't want to ask. It would stink to have to say, "No, I have the kind that doesn't have a good outcome."

"So it's leukemia?" I kept the paper in front of my face. "That's the kind of cancer you have?"

Up until that moment, the only thing I knew about leukemia is that you get nosebleeds. I'd never studied it; I just knew about the nosebleeds from growing up watching *Little*

House on the Prairie. Laura Ingalls' little brother Albert got leukemia. Oh yeah, and it was a death sentence. You get diagnosed and you die. But that was a hundred years ago. Like the paper said, things were different now.

"Yeah. They're doing a bone marrow biopsy today to figure out which kind."

That sounded painful. Should I say so? "Sounds...bad."

"I agree." He reached for the paper. "I need to keep that for the hundred other people who want all the details."

I handed it back slowly, my eyes catching the symptoms paragraph, which included headaches and fatigue and swollen gums and bone pain and paleness and weight loss and he took the paper before I could read the rest, which I was kind of glad for because it was already overwhelming. "Have you been having all those symptoms? And you hid them from us?"

"We thought maybe I had the flu. I didn't want people to worry."

I smacked his arm and then pulled back quick. "Sorry. Do your bones hurt?"

"My bones don't hurt. Don't treat me like a baby."

"Okay." I smacked his arm again. That was a non-loving touch; I could do that kind. "I tell you when I've got a mosquito bite that itches. I can't believe you've been keeping this a secret. I'm so mad at you I could spit."

"Well, don't spit on me," he said dryly. "My immune system is shot."

I deflated back into my chair and after a few seconds of heavy silence, he looked at me and said, "This is where you're supposed to tell me I'm a fighter, and I'll get through this, and everything will be fine."

"I am?"

"Everyone else has so far."

I couldn't do it. I couldn't tell him everything would be fine because I didn't know if it would. Everything felt terrible at the moment and it might get worse. "I'm abnormal," I said with a shrug.

"Knew that." He saw my face and gave that reassuring smile, the kind I was supposed to be giving him but couldn't. "Don't worry. Abnormal is a word I've heard all day long. Blood work: abnormal. Test results: abnormal. Medication reaction: abnormal. If this were a baseball game, I'd be out already."

"Chad..." I stood and gripped the bed rail. I should have gripped his hand, but if I did that, he'd know I was scared he would die and how would that be comforting?

He looked at my hand, white-knuckled around the rail. "It's okay, Vicks," he said softly. "It's going to be okay."

I didn't weep on his arm, but I came close enough that when his parents appeared in the doorway, I used the excuse to say I had to leave. Chad called to me halfway through the door and asked if I would come back tomorrow after school. I promised I would. Then I ran.

Random Fact: During a 13.5-hour surgery, physicians were able to pull out a malignant brain tumor from an 11-year-old girl's nose in Texas.

Gross.

CHAPTER ELEVEN

Leukemia. Such a technical word. I now knew how to pronounce it and define it, but I didn't know what it meant. Not really. Not in terms of turning Chad's life upside down, and maybe taking it from him.

Going to school Monday was like visiting Cancerville. I passed Alecia at her locker, surrounded by a circle of girls all hugging or crying or in general looking dramatic, and I heard Chad's name several times on my way by. I saw Dan later near the door that led to the gym. He had a basketball in hand and a frown on his face. The guys near him tossed around questions about how cancer would affect sports ability. They had gotten to pondering whether a guy could still play while doing chemo, all giving theories without any actual knowledge of the subject, by the time I was far enough down the hall to not have to hear them anymore.

Between periods I wandered to the rooms where Chad had classes that I didn't. If I was going to keep my promise and go to the hospital after school, I might as well bring his homework. He wouldn't want to get behind, and who knew how long he'd be stuck there? It was disconcerting, the power this cancer word had. Since Chad wasn't there to carry it, the word seemed to hover over me on his behalf. Every classroom I entered quieted a little, as if people had to pause whatever shallow topic they currently discussed because I had a friend who might be dying. I guess that was a good thing, maybe a respectful thing, but it sure wasn't comfortable to a girl who didn't like being even on the fringe of the center of attention.

"Sorry about Chad," some would say as I walked to the teacher's desk for assignments. Or, "I heard about Chad. I hope he'll be okay."

The ones who said things like, "He was a great guy," as if he was gone already, made me want to toss my books and run. Where was a bathtub when you needed one? Then there were the questions. All those technical ones like the adults were asking in the hospital, as if hearing some big medical words somehow made the fact that part of Chad's body was trying to kill him mentally digestible. I gave a lot of "thanks" and "uh-huhs" and a few comments about platelets that sounded intelligent. After the third room, I was sick of the "sorry" word, and I'd already collected at least four supposed natural cures random people found on the internet. Those got detoured to the trash. The last thing I was bringing Chad was some paper that implied if he'd eaten organic, this never would have happened. Like God was punishing his body for chowing down processed food but the rest of us, who ate the same junk, somehow got by under His radar.

And speaking of God, I did have one student, a friend of Chad's, come up right before I got to Mr. Seecord's class and say she was sorry, and she was praying for Chad. I expected her to move on after my mumbled "thanks," but she didn't. She looked me in the eye and said, "And I'm praying for you too. This has got to be really hard for you."

I stared at her, too surprised to say anything. She didn't pull out a paper or give me some pat saying that was supposed to fix it all. She just smiled and went on her way, leaving me with this unreasonably glad feeling that somebody out there cared. I didn't think God did, and I seriously doubted prayers to Him would help anything, but that girl cared, and that was nice.

"I heard about Chad," Mr. Seecord said when I got into the room. "Are you okay?"

Two nice people in a row. I nodded and ducked my head and found my seat, hoping no one else would say anything as I was dangerously close to looking downright emotional.

Mr. Seecord passed out papers. On his way by my desk, he leaned over a little and said low, "It's okay to grieve, Victoria."

I looked up. "There's nothing to grieve yet."

His eyes held a wisdom that I frankly didn't want. "There is," he said, and moved on.

Like a cow chews cud, I chewed on his words all morning, but didn't fully get them until lunchtime, when I walked into the cafeteria and found myself looking for Chad. He wasn't there. He wouldn't be there for an indefinite period of time. No matter what happened down the road, cancer had already changed things, was already taking things away.

I didn't want to sit with Dan and Alecia. They were surrounded by other friends and I could not handle a whole lunch period of people talking about Chad like he was their best friend when they didn't really know him.

So I found a spot far in a corner, sat by myself, and ate my sandwich while I took Mr. Seecord's advice.

I grieved.

Random Fact: The human head has around 100,000 hairs on it. Losing 50-150 hairs each day is considered normal.

So if you lose only 49 hairs a day, that makes you weird?

CHAPTER TWELVE

Chad shaved his head the next day. Said he didn't want to be pulling it out by the handfuls once they started chemo. Seeing him without hair made it all real.

The rest of the evening, I couldn't get the words to stop throbbing in my mind.

Chad has cancer.

Chad has cancer.

Chad has cancer.

Random Fact: In a study to improve hospital design for children, researchers polled 250 children regarding their opinions on clowns and every single one of them reported disliking or fearing them.

My hand's up.

CHAPTER THIRTEEN

For a week, and then two, Chad's leukemia diagnosis was a big deal. People came and went in a flurry of crisis mode activity. They reacted and cried and visited and talked about it. They flooded the Carlson's home with casseroles and fried chicken and potato salad. They prayed and they wept and they hugged.

I watched, inept at all the caring things everyone else seemed so good at doing.

And then it was like a kid who ate too much sugar after the high wore off. The energy seemed to fade out. I suppose people can only stay in crisis mode so long. This one church planned a big fundraiser, and another church that Chad had gone to summer camp with last year organized a blood drive, but even before those happened, people stopped coming to the hospital so much. The cards trickled in less and less. No more flowers arrived, though that was no hardship on Chad. He sent all the flowers home with his mom anyway. But I felt badly for him about the rest. There was this feeling about the whole thing that he should be better by now, and people didn't know what to do with the fact that he wasn't, so they went back to life and left him there with his cancer and his get-well-soon cards and a few balloons trailing the floor because the air had gone out.

I had been feeling like such a loser, just being there while everybody did these wonderful things, but when everybody else was gone, I was still there. I went to the hospital every day after school and we did our homework together. I sat next to Chad's bed, not touching him, just there, when they came to take more blood or run more tests or give him a bunch of information that didn't really tell him anything.

His family was exhausted. The nurses said they were lucky, that some kids' families lived hours away and had to either drive back and forth, or stay in motels or live in the hospital. The Carlsons were grateful, but it didn't make them any less tired. We started doing kind of a rotation. They'd come certain times, but if I was there, they felt like it was okay to go home and get some rest, or eat some of those casseroles that had been stored in the freezer because they were eating hospital food. Chad's brother, Cameron, didn't come frequently enough to make me nervous. Whenever he did, he didn't stay long. Like many others, he didn't seem to know what to talk about. If he mentioned school or ball games or anything else Chad was missing, he'd cut himself off and say sorry and then get real quiet. It was mega awkward, so then he'd leave after awhile, not so much avoiding Chad as probably avoiding the guilt he felt that his brother's life was on hold while his wasn't.

Chad himself was sometimes different, sometimes the same. He'd get a blood transfusion and be super hungry, or he might take meds and be groggy, or he might eat and feel like barf. Some days were bad. Some were good. Some days were good, bad, and everything in between, all in sections of time based on the war going on inside him and the stuff they were putting in him to fight it.

"Hey, guys," he said when the nurses were prepping to put something called a Huber needle into this port thing under his skin so they could give him chemo without having to jab him every time. "If I ask them, you want to stay and watch? It's like a big thumb tack."

I wasn't the only one in the room at the time, but I might have been the only one whose skin did not turn some shade of green. Dan left the room immediately. For a jock, he was a baby when it came to blood and stuff. Alecia waved her hands in front of her face awhile, talking nonstop for some reason about formaldehyde and last year's dissection project in science, and then said something about needing to make sure Dan hadn't passed out, and she left too.

"Chickens," Chad said. He laughed and I breathed out in relief. Had it been a down day, having friends literally run away from you would have to be hard.

"Sure, I'll stay," I said. I did not particularly like the idea of watching people thread non-physical material into a physical body, but I'd discovered lately that I wasn't the queasy type, so if Chad wanted someone with him, I'd be there. I figured if he could stand it, so could I. (If they were putting him under, that would be another matter; I'm not for watching minor surgical procedures just for the fun of it.)

"You can stay if you want," nurse Sarah informed me. She was one of the more cheerful ones and I liked her. Her scrubs had smiley faces on them. "But everything has to be sterile. You'll have to wear a mask and hair net."

"On second thought," Chad said. "I think we'll just both go out in the hall and wait with Dan and Alecia. Let us know when it's over."

A little sadness snuck into her eyes, but her mouth smiled. "If only you could, Chad." She put her gloved hand on his arm. "I wish you could."

Cancer stinks. I'd say a worse word, but I've always thought that bad words were a lazy way to avoid having to find the word that best fits. Stinks fits cancer well. Stink fills up a room and every time you breath in, it's there, and even if you leave the room, when you come back, it's still there. You can't get away from it without literally getting away, so for Chad, since he couldn't get away from himself, he was trapped. That had to...stink.

Everything was different, so I tried to stay the same as much as possible. Chad had never needed a lot of order, but I figured not knowing what was going on inside your own body had to be freaky scary, so maybe having a friend who was emotionally consistent might help. That, and there was also the truth that I didn't know how to be anything else. If he wanted a dramatic friend or a joking friend, those both came in the forms of Alecia and Dan, but I noticed they had a hard time visiting those days when Chad felt wiped out or kind of down, and since no one knew when those times would be, their visits dwindled too. I couldn't fault them for wanting their friend back the way he was, but Chad was Chad, and however he was at any given moment was him, at least to me.

For those first two weeks, I felt useless and helpless and like a failure. Then, when the chaos settled, I discovered I did have a gift to offer. A gift that mattered.

I stuck around.

Random Fact: Most lipstick contains fish scales.

I rest my case on my aversion to makeup.

CHAPTER FOURTEEN

Dan called during the Saturday fundraiser to tell me it was a huge success. He had volunteered to sit in a dunking booth, and was spending the day soaking wet and shivering for a good cause. Chad was doing well enough that day to make a short appearance. The nurses had held off on that day's round of chemo. They made him promise to put a ball cap on to protect his head from the sun and wear a mask to keep from catching people's germs, but they did say he didn't have to sit in a wheelchair the entire time. The people in charge hoped to raise a couple thousand dollars to help the Carlsons with all the medical expenses. Being sick is costly in more ways than just physical.

Not being one for big, loud events, I chose to skip it. Chad would be surrounded by energetic, caring people and that was good. He wouldn't need me that day. I went to his house instead to pick up some of his stuff so I could decorate his hospital room with it—another idea from a caring person other than me. The last time Mom visited, she mentioned how bare the room was and how nice it would be if he had some of his familiar things around him.

I wasn't sure which things would be good. Probably not any trophies or stuff that would remind him of what he couldn't at present do. I knocked on the front door and Cameron opened it. As always, I got gangly and tongue-tied the moment I was in his presence, and stood with my mouth open working to get words to come out.

"Chad's at the fundraiser," Cameron said.

I nodded. "I thought you'd be there too."

He shrugged. "Nah, all those people being cheerful and saying happy things just feels depressing to me."

That girl came to mind, the one who had told me she was praying for me. It looked like Chad's older brother could use someone saying, "It's got to be hard for you too." I'd have said it if I had the nerve. But all my nerves go limp like cooked spaghetti when I'm around him, rendering me not only useless but somewhat soggy.

I followed him inside, took my coat off, and got even more nervous thinking that his parents were probably at the fundraiser with Chad. Whether they found it depressing or inspiring, I knew they would not miss any event people were doing for their beloved son. Mrs. Carlson was probably crying at that very moment.

Cameron turned to me. "Want something to drink?"

He was probably wondering why I was there. "No, thanks. Is it okay if I go up to Chad's room? I want to get some of his stuff to take back to the hospital."

"That's a nice thing to do."

I shrugged. "My mom's idea."

He waved his arm toward the stairs. "Go ahead. You can check the basement too, but you'll probably only find socks and video games down there."

"Just video games. I cleaned up his socks the night he went to the hospital." What a dumb thing to say. I shook my head at myself and started up the stairs. It felt worse than strange, being in Chad's house without him in it. More like disturbing. His stuff was all still there, but it was missing his voice and his big grin and...

I realized I was thinking like he was gone and never coming back. I told myself not even to think the word death, and, as Mother would say, got a move on. Chad's room was the second on the left. The first room was Cameron's. I glanced in on my way by, as I always did, hunting greedily for any little hint of information about the boy Chad used to call "Camera" back when he was a baby. His parents still talk about the time they asked Chad to go get the camera for them and he came back lugging his brother in by the hand. Only now they tell it with tears in their eyes.

"Are you lost?"

I whirled and almost ran into the object of my daydreams. He was taller than the last time I'd stood that close to him, which upon recollection might be never. "Oh, uh, sorry." I skittered a little to the side to make it look like I wasn't just standing there looking into his room like a stalker. "I was thinking."

"A good use of time." His mouth curved. "What about?"

Instead of the nine or twelve things I'd been thinking about him, I choose the one that wouldn't be personally embarrassing to say. "I was thinking that it had to be hard to be a parent sometimes."

His lips dropped. He had nice lips, not too thin like some guys. "Yeah," he said, and I gave myself the luxury of watching his lips move while he spoke. That probably sounds borderline stalker-ish, but as I said, he had nice lips. And eyes. And chin. "We'll get dinner ready and Mom will yell up for Chad to come down, and then she'll start crying." He shoved his hands into his pockets. "Dad spends a lot of time out in the garage or watching TV. He doesn't like talking about it, so Mom unloads on me." He shrugged. "I don't mind, but I can't fix anything, you know? After awhile I want to go out to the garage too."

Had we been close friends, I might have reached out and touched his arm. Normal people would probably give a hug about right then, but you've probably figured out by now that touch isn't something I naturally do. It would be like trying to produce tears on demand. Forced tears look silly or melodramatic or just fake, and for me forced touches are stiff and my hands seem to get big and cumbersome and I don't know where to put them or what to do once I put them somewhere. It just gets complicated and makes me and the other person uncomfortable, so I've pretty much given it up.

Which doesn't matter because there was about as much chance of me daring to touch Cameron, of all the people in the world, as there was in me throwing my row of rubber ducks into a pond for the fun of watching them drift away from each other.

He glanced down at me. "And now I'm unloading on you. Sorry about that. You probably want to get Chad's stuff and get out of here." He went into his room and shut the door. I stood in the hallway, my eyes going unfocused on the door, making my brain see 3-D patterns. I wondered if my secret interest in Chad's big brother was because he was really that attractive, or if all of it was based on what he did that afternoon all those years ago.

Random Fact: One fourth of the bones in your body are in your feet.

None of them keep your feet from stinking.

CHAPTER FIFTEEN

Physically speaking, if there was a contest between Cameron and Chad, Chad would win on the attractive scale. Chad had the square jaw line and the hair falling over his forehead and that half-cocky grin that got girls drooling, or whatever the girl version of drooling is. Cameron did not have the kind of looks that drew immediate attention like Chad did. His attractive qualities were the kind you noticed little by little the longer you looked. He had a solid face and his eyes crinkled when he laughed, and if he ever grinned wide, his left cheek got a dimple in it. His voice was low, gravely in the morning or if he got upset, and he had a habit of rubbing his hand over his head, which would mess up his hair but he never noticed and it would stay that way until someone would go by and rub his hair back in place. Wanting to be the person to do that was a regular pastime when I was at Chad's house, but as that would involve both touching and declaring I had a crush on him, it was of course not going to happen.

The door swung open and I jumped half a foot. Cameron's eyebrows went up. "Are you...okay?" He looked down the hallway to the left and the right, then down to my feet on the carpet. It seems he did not think that me remaining in front of his door was normal, which would be an accurate assessment of the situation.

"Sorry. Got stuck thinking again." I shot him the kind of grimacing smile you give when you're caught staring at someone, then took off down the hallway and disappeared into Chad's room. I should have asked Mom to get Chad's stuff. Why did I decide to come personally and make an idiot of myself?

"You need any help in here?"

I jumped again, this time in rotation, and saw Cameron Carlson standing in Chad's doorway. His gaze dropped to my empty hands. I filled them with the first things in reach: a t-shirt draped over a chair, and a pillow that was hanging half off the bed. Chad was a lousy housekeeper. "I was thinking maybe I should clean up in here a little."

He chuckled and leaned his shoulder against the door. "He won't be able to find anything if you put stuff where it belongs."

Cameron kept his room as neat as Chad's was chaotic. Maybe that was the real reason I liked him. He came into the room and picked up random clothing items from the floor, dumped them on Chad's bed, then wadded each up and tossed them like basketballs toward a laundry basket in the open closet. The third throw knocked the basket over and as he went to right it, I saw him smile as he reached behind it to something on the floor. He pulled out a shoebox full of old match box cars. "Remember these?"

I didn't know if I should smile or turn red. The turning red part happened involuntarily. Looking at the cars, I was transported back at least ten years ago. The teachers were concerned that I didn't play well with others. I couldn't handle it when kids moved the toys I'd placed so methodically. Personally, I had found a good solution to that problem: play alone. The experts, however, did not see this as satisfactory to my development. I found out because Chad overheard my parents talking to his parents about it. They discussed homeschooling me, and Chad—bless his heart, as my mother often did—thought that school was the most fun place on earth and didn't want me to miss out. For several weeks, he came to my house every day after school and we would work at playing together. I say work because for me it wasn't playing. Playing meant I got to put my toys in perfect positions and then play with them one at a time, returning each one to its exact spot before choosing another. The kind of playing they called normal was work. Chad would move one toy. I would move it back. He'd move it again and tell me to leave it there, and I'd argue about how it wasn't right and I needed to put it back and this wasn't any fun. If that didn't work, I'd start rocking and if that didn't work, the screaming came.

Cameron set the box of cars on the floor and sat cross-legged behind it. As if he had gone back to boyhood, he took the cars out one at a time and set them on the carpet. I could not stop myself. I joined him on the floor and placed the toys in a perfect line. I knew what was coming and even though I was years past playtime, my stomach still tightened waiting for it.

Those afternoons long ago trained both Chad and me to have enormous amounts of endurance. Or stubbornness. Chad would sit out my screaming, moving that one toy out of order every time I moved it back. After awhile, I stopped screaming and the rest of my family remained in the house instead of having sudden picnics in the backyard or deciding they needed more groceries for the evening meal. Eventually, I was able to sit without rocking while the one toy remained out of order. When I could force myself not to put the toy back, a great, torturous success, he made things even harder. We started practicing at his house instead of mine.

I probably should not remember those times so vividly, since we were only five or six years old, but the experience was so traumatic for me I think it's branded on my brain forever. I'll probably be mumbling about it when I'm ancient and live in a nursing home, putting pill bottles in order and freaking out if a nurse moves one.

"You ready?" Cameron asked, and I jolted back to the present. He had set every car out. I had placed every one into a line. Slowly, just as Chad would do when we were kids, Cameron picked one car out of the line and put it at an angle next to his leg.

I felt the tension in my hands. They wanted to pick it up. Put it back. I was a kid again, fighting against my nature, telling myself I had to learn that other kids didn't play like I did. Other kids liked things to be messy. Disorderly. That was fun for them. My fun was not fun for them.

"It's still hard for you, isn't it?"

There was no judgment in his voice. I nodded and smiled as if it wasn't a big deal, which it really wasn't anymore. I wasn't breaking out in a cold sweat or containing a scream. It was just a matter of telling myself things, adapting my thoughts to the realities of other people. I picked up the wayward car, but then handed it back to Cameron and picked up one of the ones still in the row. I touched the miniature wheels and headlights, and remembered the day Chad's big brother became my hero.

Random Fact: During the 17th Century, the Sultan of Turkey ordered his whole harem of women to be drowned and replaced with a new one.

That's like a Disney princess horror movie.

CHAPTER SIXTEEN

It happened in the fall, during the first quarter of first grade. Chad and I had been practicing for an hour and I was fed up and ready to quit when Cameron came home with some of his friends. I did not notice them at first because my attention was laser focused on the little red car Chad had put not just out of order, but up on top of the living room coffee table, off kilter, with one wheel off the table suspended in air. They must have had a conversation about me but I missed it, until laughter brought my eyes from the car to the group of boys standing around me in a circle. Chad had gone to the bathroom so I was the only kid there to pick on.

"Dude, look at her," one of them said to the tallest one. "She's, like, obsessed with that car."

The tall one, who I assumed was named Dude and have thought of him as such ever since, smirked and laughed again, but I could tell it was not a nice laugh. I learned early on to know the difference when people laughed with you and when they laughed at you. "What happens if we move all the cars out of order?" He swiped a foot across our play area, knocking over and scattering most of the cars.

They pointed and joked as I frantically gathered the cars and put them back in order. Even the red one on the table. In tears, I put my head down so they could not see my face, and with precision rearranged my rows of cars first in one direction, then another, waiting for them to leave so I could go home and get in the bathtub.

Dude kicked the cars again and the others laughed, but I heard Cameron say, "Let's go play video games." He would only have been about eight years old at the time, and his voice was still young and high.

"This is more fun." Another kick. More cars awry. I could not move fast enough to protect the row. My tears were falling by then.

"Leave her alone."

"She's just a dumb kid who can't even play right," the Dude boy said. "What's wrong with her?" His voice was louder than the others. It hadn't taken two years of kindergarten for me to know that King of the Hill wasn't just a recess game. People played it in life too. Whoever got on top had to be mean and push others away to stay on top.

Dude's foot came near but then I saw another foot block it from kicking the cars again. I looked up. Cameron stood between me and Dude. "There's nothing wrong with her," Cameron said. "She's not afraid to be who she is."

I saw Dude's friends all look at Cameron instead of their king of the hill. Cameron put his hands on his hips. "My mom says nobody should have to pretend to be something they're not."

"What if what they are is not cool?" Dude laughed in Cameron's face. "They know they're dorks. They even call themselves dorks." He started chanting the word and the others followed.

"Better to be a dork than a bully and a jerk."

Everybody got quiet and waited. I even stopped thinking about the two cars that had been kicked out of my reach. He was only a kid, but I will never forget how Cameron crossed his arms and looked around at his friends. "You can go play video games if you want," he said. "I'm staying here to play cars with her." Then he turned his back on them and sat down across from me. Dude griped and led the others away. I don't know if they went to the basement to play or just went home. I did not care. Cameron and I hunted down the far-flung cars and he put them back into a perfect row for me.

I think I've been half in love with him ever since.

"Do you still have the ducks?"

I came back to the present and noticed I held that little red car in my hand. Cameron looked more like a man than a boy now, and he had run his hand over his hair and part of it stuck out to the side like someone had walked by with a vacuum hose. He returned his car back into perfect order. I put the final one in place. "Yes. They're on my bathroom windowsill."

"In a row?"

I smiled. "Of course."

He pulled one of the cars away and looked at the line, which now resembled a row of teeth with one tooth missing. "Chad was good at knowing what people needed," Cameron said. "He could always tell when our mom had a bad day. I'd find him helping her fix dinner, or writing her a little card or something. He was the thoughtful kid. The good kid. I just played video games."

I debated whether I should protest his words or the fact that he was talking about Chad like he'd died. Even thinking the word made me shudder. I packed up the cars and handed Cameron the box. "I'd better get his stuff."

We worked without words, me making choices and packing up a few things, Cameron cleaning up the room despite his suggestion not to do so earlier. Normally, I would have been over the moon happy to be doing something together, but as everything over the past weeks, this was no normal circumstance. I stole small glances here and there, but told myself to not let my thoughts wander to Cameron

Carlson. Chad needed me to be there for him, and I wouldn't if I was pining over his brother.

That was why, when Cameron offered to drive me to the hospital and us hang out in the cafeteria for awhile before going to see Chad, I declined. Chad had been there for me, day after day, when I needed more patience and unconditional friendship than most people would even try to give. I had to return that.

Now was not the time to follow my heart, even if ignoring it hurt. I left Chad's house, tossed his bag in my passenger seat, and drove alone to the hospital, wondering if Cameron would ever offer to spend time with me again.

Probably not. Even heroes have their limits.

Random Fact: The electric chair was invented by a dentist.

Add a fear of dentists to my fear of clowns.

CHAPTER SEVENTEEN

"It's Tuesday," Chad said. "Why aren't you at the graveyard?"

Alecia looked at the wall, which wasn't bare any longer since I taped up a few cards some kids had made for Chad. I hadn't asked about the tape and hoped the hospital wouldn't sue me or anything. Dan laughed Chad's question off. "Cause we're here with you, dork."

Chad turned to me, sitting in my usual chair next to his bed. "But what about the ducks? They'll be hungry."

"It's not like we're their only source of food," Alecia said. She wandered the room and looked over or picked up all the things I had brought from Chad's house, like she was in a store.

"I'll go after I leave here," I told Chad. He seemed really restless and frustrated, or, I didn't know, anxious or something. "Don't worry about the ducks."

"Are you avoiding the cemetery because I might be there soon?"

Dan and Alecia froze where they were and gave each other a look. Chad missed it because he was rolling his head side to side on the bed, but I saw guilt all over their faces. That was exactly why they'd insisted we come to the hospital that day. Going to the graveyard wasn't fun anymore. "We wanted to come see you while it was still visiting hours, okay?" I said. "I'll go feed the ducks after we leave. I promise." I'd go, and I'd feed the ducks, but I wouldn't see them much.

I'd see the stones and the names and I'd wonder about the people. How had they died? Had their loved ones been surprised? Were any of them Chad's age?

Chad pushed the call button and asked for some ice water. Alecia came close and rubbed his arm, but then pulled away. "You're all clammy," she said. She looked back at Dan, who stayed several feet away from all of Chad's tubes and needles. "He looks like he feels really bad. I think we should go."

"I'll stay," I said.

"He probably needs rest, Vicky."

"He can fall asleep with me here. He's done it lots of times." I hated the thought of him waking up with no one there.

"Maybe he wants to be left alone every once in awhile."

What was Alecia getting at? I looked at Chad. "Do you want us all to go?"

His face was covered in a sheen of sweat. Had they given him a chemo treatment that day? He was usually sick and pretty crabby those days. Maybe they upped the dose and it was affecting him a lot. "Go away," he said.

"See?" Alecia gestured toward his bed. "He wants us to leave."

"Then I'll wait in the waiting room until he's doing better." If he started feeling better in a few minutes, I didn't want him to worry that we were mad that he'd sent us away.

"Would you get a life, Vicky?" Alecia put her hands on her hips. "You're here all the time. We get that you care about him, but are you not aware how needy you look? Yes, Chad lets you cling to him and be all codependent on him, but you're not attached at the hip, okay? Can't you see he needs to rest and get better?"

Whoa. I gripped the arm rails of my chair with both hands. I looked up at Alecia, who sighed like I was dense and launched herself out of the room. Dan shrugged and mumbled something before he followed after her.

I sat in a daze. Was it true? I thought I was here because I cared about Chad, because he was my friend. Was I really here all the time for myself?

A nurse came into the room with a cup of ice water. She took one look at Chad and disappeared. I stayed in my chair, numb, while the nurse returned with two other women in scrubs. They checked Chad's forehead, punched numbers on machines, took his pulse, and even lifted his eyelids and looked under them. Their faced pinched with worry and I forgot Alecia's words in my concern.

"What's wrong?" I asked.

"He's burning up with fever," nurse Sarah said. Her scrubs had monkeys on them that day. "Was his temperature high the last time you checked his vitals?" she asked another nurse. I missed the response, but soon they were calling doctors and there was a whole lot of fussing around his bed. Chad was rustling in an almost thrashing way.

"You need to go now," a nurse told me. I couldn't seem to move. Panic glued me to my seat. She helped me up. "We're going to need to get him into ICU."

Machines started beeping as they disconnected them from Chad's body, adding to the chaos. They lowered the head of his bed until he was lying flat, and pushed the whole bed, with Chad in it, through the door and down the hallway to the left. I followed until they rushed through a set of double doors marked clearly to block out people like me.

Alecia found me there minutes later. "What happened?"

"They took him to ICU. We should call his parents right away." My tongue felt thick, like I'd stuffed a roll of gauze in my mouth.

"I'm sorry for blowing up at you back there," she said. "You're probably here for all the right reasons. It makes me feel guilty that you don't mind staying hour after hour and I do."

"Do you really think I'm codependent?" I didn't look at her, but kept my eyes locked on the DO NOT ENTER letters on the door right in front of my nose.

Her sigh was louder this time, or maybe it just echoed in the empty hallway. "I don't know. I just keep thinking of lunchtime, about how you're so lost without him there to hide behind."

Being a literal thinker, I almost protested that I hadn't hid behind Chad since third grade. But then I thought about what she said in a non-literal sense. I did hide behind Chad. Not his body, but his presence. If he was there, I had someone to talk to, someone to accept me. He was my comfort zone.

And now my comfort zone was in Intensive Care because his life was in danger, had been for hours, and I had just sat by his bed and done nothing.

"Will you call his mom and dad?" I asked Alecia.

She already had her phone out. I would still do nothing because someone else would step forward to do something. Someone always did. She started hunting Chad's number on her phone.

I turned my back on the door and the sign and the ICU and trudged down the hall, past the waiting room, past Dan, who probably asked a question or two but I didn't hear. I left the hospital and went to the graveyard, but I hadn't bought any bread. It didn't matter. I promised Chad I'd go see the ducks, not feed them. I thought back through the conversation and remembered that I had actually promised to feed them, so I left and went to the store, then returned. The least I could do was keep my promise. Without emotion, I tore off pieces of bread and threw them into the water. The ducks came. They quacked. The little ones did things Chad and I would have laughed at, while Alecia sighed at our immaturity and Dan ate and talked with food in his mouth.

But now I was alone, with the ducks and a lot of dead people. I stayed until the bread was gone, then packed up the empty bag and made my way home to sit in the bathtub and figure out what a codependent girl obsessed with order does when her comfort zone is gone and life is scattered, as if a big foot came down and kicked it all into disorder.

Chad was in ICU. I was scared, but the worst of it was, I couldn't tell if I was more afraid for Chad's sake, or my own. What kind of person did that make me?

Random Fact: In the past, when a clan no longer wanted a member in it, they would burn down their house. This is where the expression "to get fired" comes from.

Pink slips suddenly don't seem so bad.

CHAPTER EIGHTEEN

I called Mrs. Carlson the next morning after breakfast and she said Chad was still in ICU with no change, so I went to school in somewhat of a daze. All morning, Alecia's words rang in my head. I got a D on my math quiz and in history class, Mr. Seecord called my name twice and told me to pay attention.

The dreaded lunch period came too soon, and I found myself standing just inside the doorway surveying the layout of the room while kids swarmed around me and found tables to sit at. Tables with friends. Friendships they'd established long ago and probably did not want disrupted by my sudden needy presence. Alecia waved and motioned me over to her table, but I didn't move her way. Dan did. He joined the crowd around her and they all talked and laughed like nothing traumatic was happening. Maybe it was a way to cope. Maybe acting like nothing was wrong made them feel like nothing was wrong. Like Chad wasn't in the ICU. Like the friendships I'd thought would be lifelong weren't fraying apart. Like lunch was a fun event and it wasn't the hardest thing in the world to ask someone if you could sit with them.

I would not sit with Alecia. I would prove to her that I could function in life without the hedge of the four dorks around me. Quickly, I looked over the lunch room. Chad had found me, an abnormal kid, and made me feel normal. Could I do that for someone else?

There, in the far corner, I saw a guy sitting alone at a small table near the wall closest to the bathroom, where nobody wanted to sit for obvious reasons. Two long poles with handles near the ends, like canes, rested against the table. His legs jutted away from his body at unnatural angles as he sat. Words like spina bifida and muscular dystrophy came to mind, but I didn't know enough about either to guess which one he had. Taking in a deep breath, I carried my lunch across the room to his table. "Can I sit with you?"

"No law against it."

Not the friendliest greeting, but I sat and took out my peanut butter and honey sandwich on wheat bread from home. Mom was a big believer in organic peanut butter and wheat bread. I liked the peanut butter but just once I wished she'd make a mistake and get white bread. The guy didn't say a word as I ate. I tried to think of what Chad would do. He would talk to make the person feel at ease. But talk about what?

"I'm abnormal," I blurted out. He looked up from his lunch and I continued. "I freak out if things aren't in perfect order. Like when someone leaves their locker open, or when a teacher writes crooked on the board, or if kids hand in papers that aren't stacked neatly. I used to scream..." Why was I rattling on? Chad wouldn't rattle on. He'd ask questions.

"But now you don't?"

The guy's words interrupted my mental quest for an interesting question to ask. "What?"

"You don't scream anymore?"

"No. Not out loud anyway."

"So what is this?" The guy hadn't smiled since I sat down. "Find another freak and bare your heart day?"

"I'm not a freak." This was not going well. "I'm abnormal. There's a difference."

"Yeah? What's the difference?"

"Well..." Frantic mental searching didn't produce much. "Freak is always negative, but abnormal can be good. You can have an abnormally good day or enjoy abnormally fine weather."

"So we're just so cool because we're different. Is that your schpeel?" He dropped his chicken nugget onto his tray. "You need a new one."

I should have just sat by myself. "Do you think you're a freak?" I asked.

"Hey, can I sit here?"

The guy and I looked up to see a girl holding her tray in one hand while her other hand flipped a pencil through her fingers like it was a baby baton.

"Only abnormal people can sit here," the guy told her.

"ADHD," she said.

"That'll work."

She sat. "I'm Kendra. What's your name?"

"I'm Victoria, or Vicky," I said. We both turned to the guy.

"Shane," he mumbled.

Kendra stuffed a chicken nugget into her cheek and chewed fast. She grinned at Shane. "I'll tell you about my abnormal-ness if you tell me about yours." She turned to me. "And you too. You don't look abnormal."

"Really?" I glanced down at myself. "I kind of thought it showed."

She popped in another nugget and her super fast chewing made me think of a squirrel. "Maybe since I'm not normal, abnormal looks normal to me."

I forgot about my sandwich and leaned forward. "What is normal anyway? Something exactly in the middle of everything. But almost everyone is on either one side or the other, so hardly anyone in the world is exactly on normal, which means being normal is actually abnormal, and being abnormal is more normal than normal."

"To quote my mom's favorite movie," Shane said, "truly you have a dizzying intellect."

I laughed and then I felt guilty for laughing when Chad was in ICU maybe dying. For the rest of lunch, Shane told us what it was like growing up with legs that didn't work right, and Kendra told us about bouncing off the walls and all the different medications she'd been on to fit her into the normal box. Just as my turn came around, the bell rang.

"Wow, that went by fast," Kendra commented. "Usually lunch drags on forever for me."

"We didn't have time to hear much about what makes Vicky strange." Shane said. "Same time, same place, tomorrow?"

He smiled at me and I felt like I'd won some kind of award. "Sounds great," I said. I packed up my mostly uneaten lunch and headed for class, proud over what I'd accomplished rather than embarrassed, which was my usual lunchtime emotion.

Chad would be proud, too, but I would not get to tell him for a long time.

Random Fact: Cockroaches can live several weeks with their heads cut off.

Which part lives, the head or the body? Or both? Gross.

CHAPTER NINETEEN

They kept Chad in ICU for four days and nights. The second and third days were a big scare and everybody got panicky and weepy again. In ICU, you're only allowed to visit if you're immediate family, so I stayed away except to check on whether his fever was down or if the infection had spread. His parents gave numbers about platelets and talked about new treatment ideas. My parents brought pizzas for everybody in the waiting room, which I thought was pretty cool of them. And a new group arrived, circled, and prayed.

"They're from our church," Chad's mom told my mom one of the times I came with her to hang out in the waiting room while she was a "sounding board" for Mrs. Carlson.

"I didn't know you went to church," I put in. Mom sent a glare my way but Mrs. Carlson smiled over her wad of tissues.

"We didn't. I mean, we go on Easter and Christmas, but not regularly. I'm still amazed at how they have cared and helped and been so amazing ever since this started. You'd think we were the most faithful members there by the way they're treating us."

I studied this new group with interest. I had seen many of them individually over the past couple of weeks. They were the ones bringing the casseroles or sitting and holding Mrs. Carlson's hand while she cried. I wondered what the catch was. Were they shooting for brownie points with God? Maybe they got badges, like in girl scouts, for being nice to people.

I recognized the girl who had told me she was praying for me. Did she know Chad? She was talking with Cameron and he smiled at her and I admit that, regardless of it being a hospital where we're all supposed to only be thinking of the sick person, I was fighting envy big time. Why couldn't I be that comfortable talking with Cameron? Why couldn't I think of something that would get him to smile at me like that? For that matter, why couldn't I be as interesting and pretty and normal as she was?

For a moment, I imagined going over to her and saying, "Can you ask God why He made me the way I am?" That might give her a lemon to suck on for awhile, and maybe she'd stop looking up at Cameron and saying all the right things. I didn't actually know if she was saying all the right things, but it was probable. Everybody but me seemed to know what to say in a crisis. I turned mute, like a mime without all the makeup.

She wandered over my way and said hello. "I'm Tasha. You probably don't remember me."

"I do." I scratched my head. It got itchy when I was worried. "You said you were praying for me."

"I actually meant that." She smiled. "I wasn't just saying it."

"Thanks."

We stood quiet for a moment, looking over the clusters of people and listening to the hum of their voices. Tasha clenched her hands together. "I wish I was more like you," she said.

I looked around, but I was the only person nearby. "You're joking."

"No." She did a funny pulling on her fingers thing with her hands. "You're so calm. I get really nervous in groups like this, and when I get nervous I talk more. I wish I could be still and listen like you do. That's a real gift. I go on and on, and see? I'm doing it right now!"

Someone thinking my lack of ability to know what to say was a gift struck me as very funny and I laughed out loud. It caught Cameron's attention and he came over. We stood in a triangle of sorts and he asked, "What's funny? I could use a laugh."

I motioned toward Tasha. "I was standing here envying her for knowing what to say, and she thinks I'm gifted for being quiet."

"You envy me?" It was Tasha's turn to laugh. "Don't girl. My life is so far from normal. I mean, look at me."

I did. She was beautiful.

"My mom is white and my dad is black, so I ended up a creamy mocha."

"Your skin is an amazing color," I said. "And really smooth."

"Thanks." She smiled shyly. "I actually do really like the color, and I love my hair. On humid days it tightens up into these awesome corkscrew curls, and on dry days I can smooth it out. But I'm missing my point."

Cameron grinned. "What is your point?"

She blushed and it was pretty and I had this sudden, insane urge to ask Alecia to teach me how to do my hair or something. "We go to the same church as Cameron," she said to me. "Well, he doesn't really go to our church, but he came to summer camp once."

"True," Cameron said. He stood with his legs apart and one knee bent a little. I'd always been fascinated by people who can look comfortable standing up. I'm always shifting my weight from one hip to another, but then I feel off kilter and try to stand perfectly straight, which never works. I think my center of gravity is in the wrong place.

"Well, as you know," she continued to Cameron, "your church is full of white people. It's got maybe two black families in it. But it's where my mom went growing up, so when we moved back here, that's where we went. I told them I felt out of place, but they said it would build character. They're really into building character. I should have a ton of it by now."

Cameron chuckled. "Don't listen to her, Victoria. She's one of the most well-liked people at the church and at school."

"Really?" Tasha blushed again and pulled on her fingers. I was still reeling from the shock that someone as pretty and socially aware as her felt out of place anywhere in the world. "I just feel so...so..."

"Abnormal?" I offered.

"Yeah. Different."

"You should sit at our lunch table tomorrow."

"What's that?"

I smiled. "Nothing. Just a joke."

"I don't get it."

"Well, we—"

A doctor entered the waiting room and all conversation ceased as we surrounded the poor man. I hoped he wasn't claustrophobic. He told us Chad was "out of the woods" and I knew my parents would like that cliché. His fever was down to manageable and if the rest of his infection cleared up, they would put him back in his regular room the following day. I heard murmurs of relief and Cameron said, "I'm going to go get some of that pizza your parents brought. I've been starving, but just couldn't eat until we heard something, you know?"

The doctor held up his hands and we quieted again. "Chad has needed a lot of blood. A lot of blood. I heard some of you are hosting a blood drive in a couple of weeks in his honor. I just want to add my assurance that every drop counts, and giving blood saves lives." He looked back at Tasha and me, then over at Cameron digging through the pizza box. "You teenagers, if you're sixteen or older, can donate blood if you have your parents' permission. I hope you'll spread the word at school and church, and have a great turnout."

He lowered his voice and talked specifically with Chad's parents, and I found myself suddenly hungry now that Chad wasn't in danger anymore. Tasha followed me to the pizza and we each took one of the last few pieces. They were cold now and kind of hard, but pizza was pizza. "Are you going to give blood?" I asked her.

"I hadn't thought of it until now, but I guess if my parents let me I will. Will you?"

"I've never done it before, but sure, if it helps Chad. I just hope I don't pass out."

She wiped some pizza sauce off her chin with a napkin. "Yeah, I'd feel like such a loser if I fainted at one needle when poor Chad is getting stuck all the time."

"Do you really pray to God like He's there?" I knew it was off topic but I never was good at thinking of transitional things to say. "Like He's actually listening to you?"

She looked kind of surprised, like no one had ever asked her that before. "I do. I talk to God all the time. He's the only One who knows what's really going on, and He's the only One who can do anything about things like cancer, so yeah, of course I pray to Him."

"If He's all powerful or whatever, why did He let Chad get cancer in the first place?"

She smiled. "I've been asking Him that."

I knew my face was in a smirk and tried to straighten it so what I said didn't come out as totally sarcastic. "I bet He hasn't told you the answer to that."

"Not yet." She was still smiling. "But just because He hasn't told me the answer doesn't mean there isn't one."

"That would make a good saying cross-stitched on a pillow."

She laughed and as weird as our conversation was, I felt good inside. I was in public, talking with people around my age, without Dan or Alecia or Chad there to cushion my words or help people see me as better than I was. Now, it was true that during my time there I had straightened all the magazines into perfect stacks and was now organizing the pizza trash for disposal, but I hadn't run away and I wasn't even wishing I could go home to my bathtub and my ducks.

The next day, when Tasha came over to our table at lunch and asked me to explain the joke, that good feeling came again. I told her about our abnormal table. She laughed and then asked if she could join us. Kendra looked surprised but said, "Sure!" Shane looked even more surprised, but then grinned really big. I got this sense that life was full of possibilities, and perhaps, if I could start something like this, I had more courage than I knew.

When I thought of courage, I thought of Mr. Seecord and the question I'd kept inside for almost a year. Could I actually work up the nerve to ask him?

Random Fact: Earth is the only planet not named after a god.

Who decided that? Was that on purpose?

CHAPTER TWENTY

A whole week passed while I alternated between avoiding Mr. Seecord and inching toward his desk after class trying to work up that courage I thought I might have. That Friday, after nearly making myself sick over it, I gave up and life moved on. Specifically, Chad's fight for life moved on. He got out of ICU and battled migraines and nausea and a bunch of other nasty symptoms from the chemo or the cancer or the lousiness of being stuck in a hospital bed for weeks with no end in sight. There was a break in sight though. After the first five weeks of treatment, they'd let him come home for a few days, but then they would start another five week round, so if you ask me, that was about as exciting as saying, "Here, we pulled half your teeth, now you get to go eat an ice cream cone before we pull the other half. Enjoy!"

We all acted like that break would be a great thing, and Chad talked about it like he was looking forward to it, but I didn't know if that was sincere or just for our sakes. We were all getting good at talking positive in Chad's room, avoiding the bad stuff, focusing on the good stuff. After awhile, I wanted to ask for some anti-nausea meds myself.

It felt like life should be on hold until Chad could come back into it, but time wouldn't cooperate with my philosophy. Life did move on outside the hospital. I started looking forward to lunch at my abnormal table. It was fun, getting to talk about being different instead of pretending it away. The more I talked to Shane and Kendra and Tasha—who really wasn't abnormal but she thought she was—the more I realized that a whole lot of people around me felt the same way I did. Like they didn't measure up and everybody else knew how this whole life things works and they were falling behind. A couple times, I even started a conversation before or after class with someone who looked uneasy or nervous. The others at the table were teaching me nervous habits so I could recognize them. Tasha pulls on her fingers or clenches her hands. Kendra chews on her hair, which is unsanitary, but she can't get herself to stop it. Shane's foot twitches or he scratches his ear.

I started a new notebook, one solely dedicated to nervous habits. It may be weird, but I began using it as a conversation starter. I showed it to the girl who sat next to me in history, and she smiled at it and then at me, and then she told me her nervous habit was saying "like." She talked and talked, and sure enough, I heard the word "like" at least twelve times before class started. Was everybody in school as insecure as me, and I just never knew it?

I wanted to talk to Chad about it, but he was so tired and had headaches so much, I never knew if me talking would make things harder on him or easier. So most of the time I just sat quietly beside him, doing my homework or organizing whatever had gotten messy since the day before. I still went every day, but I tried to go for Chad's sake, not because I was needy and codependent.

"You've got a new notebook," he commented midway through the fourth week of his treatment. We had a week to go before the blood drive, and then two more days until his break. I was counting the days. He was probably counting the minutes. "Is it for all the dumb things people say to kids who get cancer?"

"That would be one depressingly full notebook." You wouldn't believe how many options there are of things to say that are dumb, and how many people say them. "No, I'll leave that to someone else." I opened the notebook and showed him the first page. "I'm collecting nervous habits. My favorites so far are the guy who blows his nose even when he doesn't need to, and the girl who gets hiccups and can't make them go away."

"Interesting new hobby." His words were clear today. He must be feeling better than usual. "Are you finding these on the internet?"

I shook my head. "No, I'm asking people."

"Real people? Like in real life?"

I couldn't help feeling like a kid who'd just learned to ride a bike without training wheels. I grinned at him. "Uh-huh."

"Are you sick?"

I laughed. "So what's your nervous habit?"

"Me?" He leaned back in the bed and thought for awhile. "I guess I bite the inside of my cheek. But that might be more stress than being nervous. It's pretty raw right now. But I remember doing that when Dan played his first basketball game, and when you had to do your first oral book report, and —"

"That was horrible."

"And when I tried to ask you to the eighth grade dance."

I felt myself blushing and, sure enough, I wanted to pull my knees up to my chest and rock back and forth. I needed to replace my nervous habit with a less childish, less obvious one. I tried biting the inside of my cheek but that hurt, so I pulled on my fingers like Tasha did. It gave me something to do while I tried not to remember.

Not remembering didn't work, not with Chad recounting the entire scene next to me. His voice slurred a little as he talked, a sure indication they'd given him pain meds recently and he'd be out soon. "I'd decided I had a crush on you..."

I pulled my pinkie finger, then the middle one, then my thumb, then went back and pulled the ones I missed, hoping no one would come in while he was telling this story. Neither of us had said a word about it since it happened.

"The eighth grade dance was coming up, and I couldn't dance, but I wanted to go with you. I tried to figure out how I could ask without really asking, in case you didn't want to go. No guy wants to be rejected, you know." He rolled to the side and closed his eyes, which I was glad for, because my face was certainly as red as a beet. "So I asked if you wanted to go feed the ducks, but you said it was Thursday not Tuesday, and got all buggered about it not being the right day. I was trying to get you out there without Dan and Alecia with us, but you couldn't get over it not being the right day so I gave up on that."

I felt heat creep down my neck and over my ears.

"So next I talked about the dance and how I thought it would be fun, and you said it would be awful because people would be touching. I had kind of hoped that if you liked someone, you wouldn't mind the whole touching thing, and said so. You said you didn't know, so I said we should try it out."

Forget the finger pulling. I wrapped my arms around my knees and started rocking right there in the chair.

"I knew better, but when you're thirteen I guess you're willing to try stupid things. Remember? I kissed you on the cheek." His words were coming out slower. I wondered if he would remember any of this later. "You screamed and jumped up and ran around the room in circles, and then you went to my room and found my box of cars and spent the rest of the day putting them in rows, ignoring me."

As I said, we had never talked about it since. The flame of embarrassment burned from the inside out. I stood and walked over to his bed. "I'm sorry, Chad. I've thought a thousand times about how I felt that day, but never about how you felt. That had to have been awful."

He rolled onto his back and looked up at me. His smile was adorably sleepy. "Don't worry. I figured out you're not my type anyway."

I smiled. "No, I'm not. You deserve a girl who will go with you to feed the ducks no matter what day of the week it is." I moved my hand, slow and hesitant, and put it on his lower arm.

He bent his chin to look at it, then looked at me again. "You're different," he whispered.

He dropped off into sleep, and it took all the courage I had, but I lowered my head and placed a feathery soft kiss on his cheek. "And you're wonderful."

Random Fact: The average lead pencil will write a line about 35 miles long or write approximately 50,000 English words.

But no one ever uses every bit of lead in a pencil. Now I'm sad for all the pencils in the world that will never achieve their full potential.

CHAPTER TWENTY-ONE

I was going to do it. I had touched a person on purpose. I had asked fellow students intrusive questions about their nervous habits. I had not spent any time in my bathtub—aside from actual showers—in a week.

Mr. Seecord's office was near the front of the school building, in a little section of rooms that included the principal's office, though neither of them ever seemed to be there. Like right then. It was after school, and I wanted to get to the hospital, but I had to go ask before I lost the nerve. I made my way down the hall, past the lockers—one hundred and fourteen for those who like numbers—and veered before I got to the doors to the gym on the left to Mr. Seecord's classroom on the right. He was there, wiping down the chalkboard with his one arm. All the other teachers opted for white boards but he said he liked the feel of chalk in his hand, and he liked running his fingernails down the board when the class got annoying. "Can't do that with a white board," he'd say with a smile, dragging his nails down the board and making us all cringe. It was a good tactic. Even the class clowns stayed reasonably quiet in his class. The one time Rick Jones started an argument and wouldn't shut up when Mr. Seecord told him to pipe down, Mr. Seecord had made him come stand right up at the board while he ran his nails down it. Shudder.

"Mr. Seecord?"

He turned at my timid greeting and smiled. "Victoria, come in. I'm just finishing up. How is your project coming along?"

I looked around the empty room. "My project?"

"The essay on what is worth dying for."

"Oh. That project." The one I had purposefully forgotten. "I'm still in the thinking stage." *Or rather the not-thinking stage.*

"You have more reason to think about it than most," he said. I knew he meant Chad.

"I came to ask you about Keith."

There. I'd gotten it out. Mr. Seecord went still for a moment, then sat, put his one arm on his desk, and looked me in the eye. "Okay. What about him?"

I had expected him to say we weren't allowed to talk about him, and didn't have my next question planned. I fumbled for awhile, then finally said, "You were the person he called with the threat, right?"

I knew this already, but Mom said sometimes people liked to be led toward the main question, not just hit by it like a cannonball.

Mr. Seecord nodded. He looked at me intently, like he was trying to read my mind. I didn't like it at all. "That's right."

"What did he say?"

I knew most of what he'd said from the newspaper articles, but they might have left something important out. In fact, I was sure of it, deep in my gut, and that surety was what kept me there despite being looked at so directly.

"Why do you want to know, Victoria?"

"Because of life and death," I heard myself say. I hadn't connected them in my mind before, but the project and the question were interconnected. "He called you instead of the other teachers, and I think I know why. He knew you wouldn't panic. He knew you would know how to respond, and that seems backwards. Like he wanted to be caught, or stopped." I was rambling like Tasha when she got nervous. "It doesn't make sense, but it sort of does, and I keep thinking if I knew what he really said, I could put it in the right place in my head, because right now it doesn't have a place because it doesn't make sense, and..." I stopped and took a breath and then decided to shut up and wait for him to respond.

He waited for a moment, gazing out the window like he did when he remembered Afghanistan. Then he said, "Normally, I wouldn't be talking about this at all with a student. But you..."

"I'm not normal," I said without any sting to it. For once, it was a good thing, if it got me answers.

He smiled. "You are extraordinary, Victoria," he said. "I've always thought so."

I could have basked in that sentence for a week, but he was answering my question so I had to focus.

"Keith had been struggling for quite some time. I was trying to help him, but he got beyond my reach. Some of the things he was into..." He looked away again and I wondered if he'd forgotten I was there, listening. "I suspected he'd been experimenting with drugs, and he was bordering obsessive in his addiction to violent video games. It really scared me when he started talking about a fringe cult that—" He shook his head, looked and me, and frowned. "You don't need to know about that. The day of the threat he called and told me he had planted a bomb on school property and if I didn't stop him in time, a lot of kids would die."

His words took me back to the warning bell sounding throughout the building and across the grounds, the panic of evacuating the school and even the field surrounding it. We were herded like a bunch of terrified sheep to a department store three blocks down, where we waited for our parents to push through the newscasters and cameramen to come hug us and cry and take us home where we'd ask questions that had no answers. Our parents were as clueless as we were until the nightly news, when we learned Keith had been found at his home putting guns into a backpack, and he was taken away to jail and we were safe now. No one said anything about a bomb.

"That explains the security checks and guards," I said. "And why school was closed for two days."

"Yes." Mr. Seecord tapped his fingers on the desk—his nervous habit. "They searched both days and never found it, so they decided the bomb was a bluff, but Keith wasn't the bluffing type. Since it happened, some weekends when I have a few free hours, I come over here with my metal detector and look for it. I've covered almost the entire field and most of the classrooms. A few more weekends and I'll have searched every bit of the school and can rest easy."

"You really think there's a bomb planted in the school somewhere?" Wait till I told Chad about this. He'd want to get over here with his own metal detector and hunt for it.

"I want to be sure there isn't. Even if does exist, as long as Keith is in custody, it doesn't present a danger, but I don't like the idea of some student stumbling across it years down the road. This community suffered enough that day and I wouldn't want to bring all that back." He stood and in reflex I stood too. "I shouldn't have told you that, Victoria. I'm sorry I did."

"I asked," I said.

"Was that all you wanted to know?"

"No." A bomb hadn't been in my thinking at all. "I wanted to know..." I hesitated. Would asking burden him? I didn't want to do that.

"Go ahead and ask, Victoria. I can always refuse to answer."

I licked my lips. Maybe that was another nervous habit I had. "If he had showed up that day, with his guns, what would you have done?"

I thought I knew what most of the teachers and students would have done. We would have run. Hid. Tried our best to get away and save ourselves. But he was trained as a soldier. He had faced guns before. "What would you have done?" I asked again. I waited, hands clasped in my lap, while he turned and walked to the window. Without looking down, he used his one hand to rub his other shoulder, down over the spot where his other arm should be. Then he faced me. "I would have done everything I could to protect my students. I would have gotten them into safe hiding positions if possible. I would have alerted the rest of the school if possible. And then..."

He had mentioned all things that had happened that day. Standard protocol. "Then what?"

"Then I'd have stopped him."

"From killing kids."

He nodded, his face hard. "Yes."

"How?"

"Whatever it took."

I knew then, the answer I'd always known. He would have sacrificed his life to save ours. He had made that choice already. "So for you," I whispered, "what is worth dying for is other people."

Something lit in his eyes. I think it made him glad to know someone understood. "And that is worth living for too."

It felt corny, but I wanted to salute him. I wanted to tell him he was a good man. A good teacher. I said, "Thank you," and hoped he knew I meant more than just thanks for answering my question.

He walked me to the door. "Don't tell people about the bomb threat, okay?" The door had remained opened while we talked, school rules, and he put his hand around the knob to close it behind me. "It wouldn't be good to start a panic over something the police already searched for and didn't find. They think there isn't one, and I hope they're right."

"Okay." He started to close the door but I turned and asked, "Can I tell Chad?"

His frown deepened. "Do you think that would be wise?"

"Maybe not," I said with a shrug. "But it would be a distraction on a bad day. And besides, I've never been able to keep a secret from him my entire life, so I'd feel bad promising you I wouldn't tell when I know I would."

He gave me a reluctant smile. "Well, you get an A for honesty at least. Okay, just Chad. But that's it."

I smiled back and the door closed. I stood still for longer than a normal person would in front of a closed door, but I wanted to just feel it for a moment. I had done it. I had accomplished something I'd wanted to do for a long time. However small, it was a success.

I couldn't wait to tell Chad. On to the hospital.

Random Fact: Your fingernails and toenails grow after you die.

I looked that up and they actually don't grow, they just look like they do because the body dehydrates and shrinks away from the nails, creating an optical illusion of growth.

Lesson in that—don't believe every random fact you find on the internet.

CHAPTER TWENTY-TWO

"Hey, dork," I said.

I had gotten used to Chad's slit-eye, sleepy/drugged look and was surprised when he opened his eyes all the way and looked at me. "Vicks."

"Congratulations on getting out of ICU. Did they put you in the recliner as your reward?"

He patted the armrests of the hospital chair, which should not be confused with a comfy house recliner. Even still, for Chad, I'd make a big deal out of anything positive. "It's the first day in a week I haven't felt like hurling every time I turn my head, so they thought I'd like to sit up for awhile."

I smiled away my inward nausea. Disgust for throw up is probably natural, but mine goes beyond that. I gag when people just talk about it. "So do you?" He shifted and I caught his blanket as it fell off his legs. I put it back without touching him.

"Do I what?"

"Like sitting up."

"It's a very exciting experience," he said. "Like a roller coaster."

I put my backpack on his bed and sat next to it. "Want your homework?"

"Might as well." He coughed, winced, and grabbed his ribcage. "It'll keep me busy while I wait to die."

I handed him today's history paper and tried to dispel the panic suddenly flooding me. "Don't say that, Chad."

"Why not?"

"Because..."

"Because it might be true?" He sat up. The blanket fell off again but he didn't notice and I didn't pick it up. "I've been here four weeks, Vicks, and you know the one word I haven't heard the entire time? Death. Any version of it. Die. Died. Dead. Nobody will say it. Everybody pretends it's not hanging over me. Most people can't even get themselves to say cancer."

What should I say? What should I say? "Everybody wants to help you stay positive, I guess." He stared me down with that look that said we were both smarter than that. It was impossible to win a staring contest with a guy gone bald over chemo. "Nobody likes thinking about it," I finally admitted, "so we pretend it's not a possibility."

"Exactly." A little corner of the blanket remained on his right foot. He kicked it off. "But I can't pretend it away. I lay here in bed all day and all night with nothing to do but think. And it's there, Vicks. Just once I want to talk about it being there. I want to be able to say it out loud without people falling apart on me, and making me feel bad, and then I have to reassure them." He closed his eyes. "I'm so tired of trying to make everybody else feel better about this."

It was true. I'd seen him do it at least twenty times. His parents would come in and he'd put on a good face and say positive things. Dan and Alecia would visit and he'd joke with them and put them at ease. I knew it meant something that he'd chosen to bring this up with me. "Okay," I said, my heart pounding in my ears. I hoped it would drown out the sound of his voice, because I didn't want to hear the word any more than anyone else did. "You can say it to me."

"I might die, Vicks." He opened his eyes and looked at me, and I blinked away tears. "This cancer might kill me. No matter how hard I fight or how much I sleep or how much chemo I can endure, leukemia might win and I might lose. And it feels stupid to sit here in this much pain and pretend that I'm definitely going to get through it and have a long life ahead of me. This might be it. I might be living the last days of my life here in this chair or that bed." He pointed. "You shouldn't be sitting on it, by the way. Germs and all."

"Mine or yours?"

"Yours. My immune system is compromised and you might have brought in all sorts of evil bugs."

I scampered off the bed like I had the plague, which made him laugh. "Thanks, Vicks."

"For getting off your bed?"

"For letting me say it."

All the moving around helped keep me from crying. I put my backpack on the floor and shook out his sheet, willing the evil bugs to lose their grip and go flying. "You're welcome."

"I don't want to die," he added.

"Good to know."

"I just don't want to not be ready if I do, you know?"

With a grunt, I pulled the one other chair in the room around the bed so I could sit facing him. "Not really. I've never thought about being ready to die."

"Well, believe me, having cancer will make you think about it." He reached over to his bedside table and picked up a Bible. "My parents have started going to church all the time. I thought it was a cop out and said so to the pastor when he visited." He set the Bible in his lap.

I had to laugh. "You actually said that?"

"It was a bad chemo day." He smiled. "I told him God probably got annoyed being a crutch people leaned on when they were in trouble."

"Blunt."

"You can get away with a lot when you have cancer."

I propped my feet up on the footrest of his recliner. "Is this okay, or are my foot germs too close to yours?"

"It's okay."

"So what'd he say?"

"The pastor? He said that people always need God, but sometimes it takes something big to make them realize it."

I didn't bother to hide the sarcasm. "Like cancer?"

"Doesn't get much bigger than that, I guess, for a parent." He shifted again. I wanted to give him some pain meds. "And the patient." He flipped through the pages of the Bible in his lap. "I told him about our project, the essay on what's worth dying for. He gave me this Bible and said I would find a lot of answers in it, and a lot of questions."

"What does that mean?" I put my head back and closed my eyes. Four weeks of visiting and I was sick of seeing the machines and the tubes and the cards people had given him back at the beginning. And I could get up and walk out. Chad had to be going stir crazy. (I looked up that idiom once after Mom said it and found out that stir is an old word for prison, which made the phrase very appropriate for the setting.)

"I don't know, but I plan to find out," Chad said. "I'm going to read it." I heard the shuffle of pages but kept my eyes closed. "Cover to cover. It's not like I'm too busy or anything."

"Let me know if you get it all figured out."

"I will. Have you decided on yours yet?"

"My what?" I was fighting feeling stir crazy myself.

"What's worth dying for?"

"No." I could not handle hearing that word in any form one more time. "That reminds me, I need to tell you about Keith and a bomb."

Fortunately for my sanity, that distracted him. We spent the rest of my time arguing over whether there was a bomb secretly implanted somewhere on the school property, and where it would be. I almost said we'd search for it together once he got out, but didn't want to chance starting up the I-might-not-make-it conversation again. When his parents showed up, I made my escape. My last view as I walked out the door was Chad in the recliner, Bible open, his parents praying beside his chair.

Everybody I knew was turning into a stranger.

Random Fact: Phobophobia is the fear of having a phobia.

Those people have nothing to fear but fear itself.

CHAPTER TWENTY-THREE

Lunchtime used to be a mild form of personal torture, but over the next week, it morphed into the most enjoyable part of the school day. Shane came out of his shell and turned out to be really funny. He named our table the freak table, and since I had grown up proudly calling myself one of the four dorks, I had no problem with the title. Tasha must have spread the word about it, because we found ourselves frequented by visitors. Some would sit with us, others would drop by just to tell us their nervous habits for my collection, or whatever about them felt abnormal. I discovered I was, ironically, not nearly as abnormal as I always thought. Everybody who came had something about themselves that made them feel inadequate or out of place or weird. Who knew?

I was not aware how much newfound confidence this knowledge gave me until the day of the blood drive. It was scheduled for two days before Chad's first five-week break. The church people had gone all out—they had cookies and drinks and made signs that the youth group put up all over town. Tasha facebooked about it every day and they made announcements at school. I got caught up in the excitement. I mean, how cool is it to think of letting somebody suck some of yourself out of you and use it to save someone else's life? And then your body makes up for what you gave up, so it's like you sacrificed, but then you got it back. There had to be some deep meaning in that.

The blood drive started at nine a.m. and I arrived around ten. The place was swarming. I wondered how many of us were donating blood that would actually end up in Chad's body at some point. Most of the blood wouldn't be the right type, and would be used for other people, but I had the same type as him. Giving blood finally felt like I was doing something genuinely useful, a noble feeling that died fast when they sat me next to Dude and his cronies. I saw Cameron making the rounds at chairs nearby, thanking people for coming. Was he still friends with these guys? I felt like I was six years old again and hoped the nurse would stick me and get my blood quick, or maybe they wouldn't notice I was there.

Dude—I still didn't know what his real name was—made dumb comments and hit on the nurse. It was obvious he was nervous and trying to act like he wasn't. "We're offering our superior genes to the lesser mutations." He laughed liked he'd said something actually funny and of course all his little disciples laughed with him. It sounded about as canned as a sitcom, which probably meant they hadn't understood a word.

"What do you mean?" Cameron walked up behind Dude's chair and I knew he had heard and understood. Dude turned red, but got that tight-lipped stubborn look toddlers get when they get busted with chocolate all over their mouths but they're going to say they didn't eat anything.

"You know, from that book that says people who get cancer are just evolutionary mistakes."

I watched Cam's hands tighten into fists. Mine already were, but that was because I was trying to pump the blood out faster so I could get up and away from the conversation. "What book is that?" Cameron asked.

Dude didn't turn his head to look back at Cam. The nurse plunged the needle into his arm. His face went a little pale. I wanted to ask if his superior genes were feeling woozy. "I don't remember the name."

"Did you read the book?"

"No. I watched the movie."

"You're a hypocrite then." For a second, I thought the words had only gone through my head, as usual, but Dude and all the surrounding buddies looked at me like they'd look at a girl who was normally quiet to the point of being invisible, who just up and challenged the words of Mr. It himself.

Dude's face was still pale, so when he turned red, it mixed to a kind of washed-out pink. Like a cancer ribbon left out in the sun all day. "What did you say?"

I finally got why Chad enjoyed debating. The idea of intellectually shutting this guy down was very appealing. "If you really believed in evolution and random selection, you'd have to go for survival of the fittest."

"Yeah. So?"

"So anybody who truly believes in survival of the fittest doesn't give up their own blood to help the weaker members of the species."

The guy next to Dude said, "Is she talking about what happened to the dinosaurs?"

Apparently the word numbskull could be a literal term.

Cameron stepped forward and put his hand on the back of Dude's chair. Dude got a little nervous shake to his free arm, but I could see that Cam's eyes and his interest were on me. "You don't think evolution is a viable theory?"

I'd made up my mind on that long before Chad became what anyone could call a mistake. "I believe in intelligent design."

Dude's friend didn't let up. "What about the dinosaurs?"

I ignored him and talked to Cam. "Science is supposedly all about what we can observe and calculate, right?"

"Uh..." the friend said. Cameron nodded.

"It's a well-known scientific fact that all things go from order to disorder. Nothing in nature goes from disorder to order, which is evolution's main claim. Just look at a yard left untended." I smiled. "Or Chad's room."

Cameron was following me. I didn't care if the others were. "Also, since we can logically reason that anything in our observable world that has been designed has to have a designer, it's only reasonable to conclude that the order of the universe around us and even within us originated from something of higher intelligence than itself."

I was proud of my little speech until Dude smirked at me. "She knows how to use big words now," he said to the numbskull friend. "Not bad for somebody who failed kindergarten."

One of Chad's favorite defenses came spurting out of my mouth. "That's an immature debate tactic."

Numbskull looked to Cameron for translation. "A what?"

I helped him out. "When a person can't think of an actual fact to help win an argument, an immature person will switch to attacking something about them personally to deflect the audience's interest away from the fact that they have nothing of value to say."

Dude's washed-out pink flushed to more of a nineties hot pink. Cameron chuckled. Numbskull guy gave one of those laughs in case what I said was funny, he didn't want to look like he didn't get it.

The nurse lady removed the IV from my arm and I bent my elbow to hold the gauze in place until she could tape it down. "You're all done," she said, and gave me a wink. She must have been listening. For a moment I enjoyed this rare feeling of emotional superiority over someone I'd been scared of as long as my memory existed. I should have talked to him years ago.

"I think everything started with the Big Bang," Numbskull said.

"Okay." I wiggled my head a little to see if I felt faint. I'd never given blood before and didn't want to be one of those people who stood up and then wiped out on the floor. "But for something to explode, there has to be something there first. What was there to explode?"

"Uh..."

"We all came from lower life forms that evolved over millions of years." Dude was getting his needle pulled out and winced. He'd broken out in a sweat and I tried not to feel a sense of satisfaction that he looked in much worse shape than I felt. "Don't be stupid."

"Yeah," Numbskull added to me. "You're not smart enough for that."

I tossed Cameron a look. Why had I been so intimidated by these guys?

He was looking back. "You want to go for a walk?" he asked.

"Not yet, thanks." I pulled my sleeve down over the gauze and band-aid and smiled. "I'm enjoying this conversation on how I was made by intelligent design but Dude came from an amoeba."

Cameron hadn't put any food into his mouth, but he seemed to suddenly choke a little. Numbskull belted out a big laugh and punched Dude in the arm. "She just called you an amoeba!"

Dude stood, holding his arm. He wobbled a bit, and sat down again. His face was white but his eyes glared black. All the other friends stayed silent. They watched him with what I could only describe as fear on their faces. Slowly, he rose from his seat and towered over me. Another immature tactic, I wanted to say, but I kept quiet. For the first time, I realized how small he really was, and I wanted to think on that for awhile.

"So, little Victoria," he said, his voice harsh in the way I'd noticed he got when someone didn't give him his way. "Do you still line up your blocks in perfect order like a baby?"

Numbskull laughed again, but he was the only one.

"I grew out of that," I said easily, then let my own voice go soft, but still loud enough for his friends to hear. "Will you ever grow out of your need to put other people down so you feel better about yourself?"

Random Fact: At some point your parents set you down and never picked you up again.

True, but weirdly disturbing.

CHAPTER TWENTY-FOUR

People got up or sat down or pretended not to hate needles all around us, but I kept my eyes on Dude's and he kept his on mine. I'm not sure exactly what happened in those few moments, but whatever war we fought, I won. He turned away, clutching his arm like an injury. "Let's get out of here, guys," he ordered. "I'm done with this scene."

They followed, like a disorderly gaggle of geese, several of them looking back at me before filing out of the room. Numbskull stuck his hand back into view and gave me a thumbs up. I laughed and my gaze trailed back to Cameron, who had not moved from his place behind Dude's chair. He also had not stopped looking at me. I stared at his hand resting on the chair, my typical awkwardness returning in full force.

"You said intelligent design," he said, coming around the chair to sit on it. That put his knee close to mine. Funny how I hadn't noticed that Dude's knee had been that close. He might have even bonked mine once or twice now that I thought about it. "So you believe in God?"

I talked to his knee. "Chad's been reading a little of the Bible to me this week. He says that everything about it is God having purpose in people's lives, even the bad stuff." I pulled up my sleeve and slowly tugged on the band-aid. "That sounds a lot better than his cancer being some random accident that doesn't mean anything." I looked around. "If it doesn't mean anything, then why are we all here?"

"I guess all the stuff we're doing for Chad is kind of a slap in the face of random selection." He watched me nudge the band-aid. "Want me to rip that off?"

"No. I prefer slow lingering pain to one big burst of it."

"It hurts watching you."

"Then stop watching."

"I can't." He grinned. "Your methodical, pain-inducing process is mesmerizing."

For some ridiculous reason, that made me feel attractive. I pondered the ludicrousness of that while peeling the final portion of band-aid off and pulling the gauze away from my skin.

"You're going to have a big bruise," Cameron commented.

"They had to dig around to find my vein."

"Did I mention I have a weak stomach?"

If we'd been six-year-olds, I'd have tossed my band-aid at him to see if he'd freak out. But, having just waxed eloquent about immature tactics, I decided to go for a higher approach. Flattery. "At least you haven't gone ghost white like your Dude friend."

"He's not a friend." Cameron stood and waited while I hunted down a trash can for my band-aid. "And by the way, you standing up to him was very cool. You realize you kept me from having to break his nose, don't you?"

I imagined Cameron throwing a fist into Dude's face. "That's kind of a shame." My voice trailed down to almost nothing. "I owed you one from a long time ago." Did he remember? He'd probably forgotten. That day wouldn't mean much to him, not like the everything it had meant to me.

He cocked his head and looked over at me long enough for my stomach to go jittery. I put my hand against it. We walked to the open doorway and I leaned against the frame.

"You going to be okay?" He looked back into the room, probably scouting for nurses who could come to the rescue if I fell over, or threw up.

I nodded but stayed put until my insides settled down again. Blood, IVs and bruises I could handle, but one measly interested look from a guy—this guy—and I was in danger of swooning like some Victorian girl who'd forgotten her smelling salts.

Eventually I removed my physique from the stability of the architecture and we walked through the parking lot. "Thanks for coming," he said. "For Chad." He gave me that look again and I used my hands to fan my heated face. "He's lucky to have a friend like you."

Was he? "Luck didn't have anything to do with it." I shrugged self-consciously and opened my driver's side door. "He chose me a long time ago. Now I'm choosing him."

I realized how romantic that sounded and literally bit my tongue.

Cameron had his head to the side again. He looked at my face and nodded once. "He chose well," he said. He held the door open for me and I tried to think of some way to say I wasn't interested in Chad that way. I was interested in him. But how does a girl go about saying that without really saying it, because really saying it would be setting me up for major embarrassment if he turned and ran away?

I sighed and got into the car. "Things definitely go from order to disorder," I mumbled.

"What was that?"

"Nothing." I started the car. "See you around, Cameron," I said, but I doubted I would.

Random Fact: Your left lung is smaller than your right lung to make room for your heart.

A lot of things in life have to make room for your heart.

CHAPTER TWENTY-FIVE

The day finally came. Chad had endured five weeks of treatment and was getting a vacation before the next round started. We all came over that Saturday morning to keep him from being too antsy while he waited to get released for four whole days. Dan wanted to take him to a ball game. Alecia wanted to go see a movie. I wanted to feed the ducks or hang out in the basement like the old days, but I didn't say so. This was Chad's weekend. Whatever he picked would be fine with me.

We'd made an agreement with his parents. We got him all afternoon, but he would spend the evening with his family. That morning in the hospital as we laughed at the same jokes Dan had been telling for years, I stepped back a little and enjoyed things being like they once were. The four dorks. Friends forever.

That's when I saw it. It was on their faces, all three of them. They were all faking it. Even Chad. All three of them were pretending to have fun so the others would have fun. Had it been this way for a long time, and I just hadn't seen it?

When had we stopped having anything in common to talk about? How long had it been since we'd wanted to do the same things?

I looked at us and stopped seeing four ducks in a perfect row. I saw four individuals who had drifted apart.

Pretty Alecia, who wanted to be popular.

Talented Dan, who wanted to win.

Scared me, who wanted to feel safe.

Good Chad, who wanted to help.

Suddenly it all became clear. The problem with the four dorks wasn't that we were growing up and changing. The problem was me. I was the one holding everyone else back. Alecia and Dan could both be what they wanted if they weren't so bound to a friendship they'd chosen out of kindness all those years ago. And Chad, he couldn't win, because helping me feel safe meant not helping the others move on.

I knew what I had to do. "Don't go anywhere for awhile, okay?" I said, heading out the door. "I'll be back."

Ignoring their questions, I rushed down the hall and out to my car, raced home, and ran upstairs to my bathtub. There they were, as they should be, four rubber duckies in a perfect row on the windowsill. They had kept their place for nearly ten years, never changing, putting order into my world.

"It's time," I said aloud. Before I could talk myself out of it, I reached across the bathtub and took the ducks from their places. I stuffed them in my backpack and ran back down the stairs, outrunning my thoughts and then keeping them away by reciting the list of nervous habits I'd memorized from my notebook. I had found it was nice, thinking about oddities that weren't my own. I'd even started adding a second question after I asked people about their nervous habits. Once they told me what they were, I asked them what made them happen. What made them nervous? I was surprised every time at the things that discomfited people. It was a big deal to learn there were all kinds of things other people were afraid of that I didn't struggle with. It made the things I did struggle with not seem so daunting.

That's what I told myself as I slowed my steps nearing Chad's room. I knew later I would be calling myself all sorts of names and wanting to scream about this, but it was the right thing to do. And over the past couple of weeks I'd learned that I could do things I didn't feel like doing. I could go beyond what I thought I could.

They all turned when I entered the room. Dan. Alecia. Chad. The three people who had been my world. I didn't want to make a big ceremony of it, so I just took the ducks out of my backpack and set them on the bed.

I could tell Alecia tried to keep from rolling her eyes, which to me was an assurance that this did, indeed, need to be done. I picked up one duck and flipped it over to see the name on the bottom. "Dan, this is yours. Have a great life. I think you'll be an awesome basketball player." I handed it to him and he held it like a teenage guy would a rubber duckie, all uncomfortable and looking around for someplace to put it. The next one was Alecia's. "Here, Alecia. Thank you for everything. I can't tell you how much it has meant to me that you chose to be my friend."

"What are you doing, Vicky?" She took the duck and held it in both hands. Her fingernail polish was purple that day.

"I'm letting you go," I said. "It's time." I handed Chad's to him. He was still lying in bed, so I had to lean over to give it to him. Then I picked up and held mine. "You don't have to stay in a perfect row anymore. You can go."

"I don't get it," Dan said.

"Are you saying you're okay with us not being the four dorks anymore?" Alecia asked. "Really?"

"Really. Go be with all those friends who like shopping with you and stuff."

"Oh, Vicky!" She hugged me, then jumped back when I got all stiff. "Sorry. I've just felt so bad. You're sure? I mean, I noticed you've been having fun at the freak table, and you haven't looked like a lost puppy in the hallways lately, and— oh man, I'm sorry, I shouldn't have said that."

"The freak table?" Chad asked.

"Hasn't she told you about that?" Alecia was squishing her duck and I wanted more than anything to take it from her hands and set it someplace where it would be safe. Everybody had their duck in hand and I knew it was a good thing, but it was hard, hard, hard not to snatch them back and put them in a row again. Alecia flitted around the room, as much as one could flit in about three feet of open space. "We can tell you about it on the way to the movie. Or wherever we're going. I don't even care. Let's just have one last magical weekend together."

Dan looked at Chad. He did a little girly motion and laughed. "So what would feel magical to you to do first?"

"My vote is to go wherever I can get a huge strawberry milkshake," Chad said, "and onion rings."

I smiled at Dan. I had to stop looking at Alecia because her fluttering was making me dizzy. "Why don't you two go on ahead to the Swirly Cone and we'll meet you there?"

Alecia put her arm through Dan's, clearly happy with the idea. "Don't you want us to stay and help you...get him ready or something?"

"No, you can help by ordering his food so it's ready when we get there."

I was relieved when they left and it was just Chad and me. Chad slowly sat up and held his duck between his knees. "So this is the end of the four of us? You're letting all of us go?"

"Do you want to go?" I sat beside him. "I don't think I even know who you are outside of being my friend. If that's gone, who are you? What do you care about? Do you wish you could be free from the whole thing?"

"I haven't been stifling myself to babysit you all these years, or whatever weird notion you've gotten into your head lately. Just because Alecia and Dan have changed some doesn't mean our friendship was all a lie."

I flicked the bill on his duck. "When did you learn to read my mind?"

"I wish I could." He set his duck up on the windowsill. "So now my duck is alone?"

I shook my head. "Not a chance." Purposefully, I set my duck next to his.

"They're not in a row," Chad pointed out.

"No, but they're together." I smiled. "That's even better."

Random Fact: Twenty-five hospitals in North America and Europe have visual messages strategically placed near the ceilings in operating rooms. These messages are only visible when read from above, and are part of an ongoing study to test the validity of people claiming to have out of body experiences.

If you can read this...we believe you.

CHAPTER TWENTY-SIX

The magical weekend did not last. We spent the day together and then Sunday morning Chad went to church with his family. Sunday afternoon, his mom noticed a sore on his foot and said they should probably mention it to the doctor, just in case. By Sunday night, he was back in the hospital. Over the next five days, he developed a fever that wouldn't go down. They tested him for pneumonia, for meningitis, for other things I'd never heard of. They'd try one medicine and then have to give him three other meds to deal with all the terrible things the first medicine caused.

The sixth day the doctor decided to do a spinal tap to make sure no cancer cells had developed in Chad's spinal fluid, but he had to give up after trying to get in four or five times. I had just arrived and Cameron was about to leave when the doctor announced they would try again tomorrow. Chad actually cried. In front of us all. He begged them to wait. His throat was raw from the tube they put down it. He had a migraine. He was nauseated. He curled up like a kid and put his pillow over his face and the doctor ushered Mr. and Mrs. Carlson out into the hall to "talk further about their options." I heard the doctor say there was an infection raging in Chad's body and they needed to fight it. They would transfer him to

ICU again, give him heavy doses of three kinds of antibiotics, and see if they could get his fever down. I moved past where Cameron stood next to Chad's bed and eavesdropped unashamedly at the door until I finally heard the doctor say they would put off the spinal tap until they got the infection under control and his throat could heal.

"They're going to wait, Chad," I said, returning to his bedside and tugging a little on his pillow. "It's okay. You can rest. They won't do it again tomorrow."

Cameron gripped Chad's bed rail with both hands. He stared at his brother, eyes rimmed with red. When Chad stopped crying and fell asleep, Cameron released his grip and left the room.

I followed him down the hallway and out into the cold night air. He paced to the edge of the parking lot, then turned to pace back and saw me. "Go back inside, Victoria."

"Are you okay?"

"No," he said. "Are you? Is anybody?"

I'd memorized a phrase Tasha said that I liked. "What can I do for you right now?"

"Nothing. Leave me alone. Go back to Chad."

"He's sleeping. And they're taking him to ICU. They won't let me in ICU."

He waved me away. "Then go home."

I wanted to pretend to be a doctor and say, "Tell me where it hurts," but some hurts ran too deep to pinpoint. I wished for something to say, then thought of Tasha envying my ability to be quiet. "I'm a good listener," I said, walking toward him.

He turned away from me and lifted his face to the sky. "I hate it, okay?" he nearly shouted, then his shoulders dropped. "I hate this. This waiting. Waiting for him to get better. Waiting for him to die. Waiting for something to happen that decides it one way or the other so I can feel the pain and deal with it. This middle place..." He ran a hand over his head and his hair stood up in the middle. Chad's hair always stayed in place when he ran his hands through it. But now Chad was bald so that was a moot point.

Why was I even thinking about that?

Cameron leaned against the nearest car, which thankfully did not have an alarm, and put his head in his hands. It was a painful thing to see. "I hate what a jerk I am, that I can't just be strong and stick it out and be all positive for his sake. And Mom's. And Dad's. And even myself. It just—it hurts seeing him wait and wait and be in such pain, and every day there's something, but nobody knows if this is the big thing or just another little thing, even though it's big. It's like when you're sick as a dog inside and you just want to throw up and get it over with."

Slowly, like I was afraid to, which I was, I reached out my hand and lightly set it on his shoulder. He wouldn't know the significance of the fact that I was actually touching him, but I did. My hand shook and he looked up at me. His eyes were wet. "And now I hate myself for telling you. I don't want him to die, Victoria. I want him to live. To get better." He stood and faced me. "But the idea of them putting him through so much just so he can stay and be in pain for a little while longer..."

"I know." My hand stayed on his shoulder as he stood. I was not sure if I should remove it or not, so I left it there. Me not being a natural toucher showed. My elbow jutted out, like a mannequin someone had positioned.

"Not you." He shook his head. "You're the one person who hasn't fallen apart through this whole thing. You're amazing. I see you in there hour after hour and you don't lose it."

I didn't want to tell him that I was breaking on the inside; I just didn't know how to show it like most people.

He sighed. "We're all just so..."

"Tired." I knew. Oh, did I know. And if we felt this way, tired of the waiting and not knowing and hurting, how did Chad feel?

Cameron dropped his head and I don't know if it was purposeful or accidental, but it came to rest against my hair. I froze and felt my eyes go big and round, so I shut them. I told my heart to slow down. Told my lungs to fill and expel air. Kept my hand on his shoulder.

His breath came down and touched my face and I was surprised to find I did not dislike the feeling. He was all over my personal space and I was tense, but not in a bad way. My fingers curled around his shoulder as if they knew what they were doing. He said softly, "I guess you're the one who loves him best right now. The rest of us aren't strong enough."

My hand dropped to my side. "Loves him?"

He pulled away and put his hands in his pockets. Saying it must have been as uncomfortable to him as hearing it was to me. "You've probably been wanting to go. It's been a long day."

I didn't want to go, but my newfound realization that I wanted to hug him made me so uncomfortable, I mumbled something vaguely appropriate for the situation and left.

Cameron didn't seem to understand that I could sit for hours and hours well, I could do nothing very well, but when it came to saying or doing something that mattered, I was hopeless.

Random Fact: If you keep a goldfish in the dark, it will eventually turn white.

I think this has deep metaphorical meaning, though what the meaning is eludes me.

CHAPTER TWENTY-SEVEN

Chad made it through that crisis, and the one that followed a week later. Halfway through his second round of treatments, the doctor came in with surprisingly good news. He was needing less blood transfusions. His platelets were up. No infections loomed on the horizon. He talked about Chad's ANC number and Segmented Neutrophils and BANDS and white blood cells and multiplying by ten, and Chad's parents nodded along with him because by then they knew what all that mess meant.

Not me. I was still in a haze about the cancer details. I just showed up when Chad was not in ICU and stayed away when he was. I kept going to school, collecting nervous habits and making a few new friends. I procrastinated on Mr. Seecord's essay, hoping if Chad was still in the hospital by the time it was due, he'd let me off the hook.

Cameron and I kind of avoided each other in general. I think he was embarrassed and I was shy. The days blurred into a strange new normal.

Then one day I came into the room and Chad wanted to talk. It felt odd. I'd gotten used to sitting quietly while he rested, or watching movies together because it hurt too much or he was too weak to have a conversation.

"I've been thinking about what Mr. Seecord said." Even his voice sounded better. I wanted to be pleased but instead felt wary. Was this burst of energy he felt a good thing or a bad thing? "That sometimes the right choice isn't the safe one."

"That sounds like something Jesus would say."

Tasha had walked in without me noticing. She smiled at us both and curled up in the recliner on the other side of Chad's bed. "I guess Mr. Seecord would know a lot about it. He's talking about self-sacrifice, right?"

"I think so," Chad said. He ran his fingers over his scalp, like he used to run them through his hair. "Taking risks for the greater good, giving up yourself for someone else, he's always talking about stuff like that."

"I wish I had him for history." Tasha pulled out her homework. She'd been joining us a couple afternoons a week lately. "Mrs. Reese just rambles on about Greco-Roman columns and ancient ruins."

"So what did you mean, it sounded like something Jesus would say?" Chad asked.

She got that happy we're-going-to-talk-about-God look in her eyes and I reached for my backpack to get my wallet out. "I'm going to go grab a bag of chips out of the vending machine. Want anything?"

They both shook their heads, in their own new world that did not include me. Tasha started talking about how Jesus said there was no greater love than giving your life for your friends, and I left the room feeling like a third wheel. If you're a tricycle, a third wheel is a good thing. If not, a third wheel is like one training wheel stuck on a bike. It knocks you off balance and you just want to get rid of it.

Chad was finding God and I wasn't part of that. He tried bringing it up a couple of times, said he'd started working on the essay for Mr. Seecord because he was finding the answer to what was worth living and dying for, but I always changed the subject. I had lived for my friends, lived to hold us together, and now that was changing but I wasn't ready to replace it. Not yet. And certainly not with a God I didn't understand, who was somehow gaining Chad's allegiance even though He hadn't taken His cancer away.

On my way back to the room, I could hear Tasha laughing at something Chad said. Her voice sounded like bells. They were having a good time. I didn't want to interrupt with my questions or my developing cynicism about life. I had to go back into the room long enough to get my stuff together, but then I told them I had to go, and made my exit.

For some reason, talking about God gave me that same scary, tight feeling as talking about death. Chad had said once that people should talk more often and more freely about death, it being one of the few things common to every human on the planet. But I wanted to remain with those people who turned away from reality and figured if they ignored it long enough it would go away. Maybe I felt the same way about God.

I went home and spent the evening playing Mario Brothers with Alex. He creamed me, which made him happy. After Mom took him up to get ready for bed, I hung out with Dad awhile. He had two new metaphors to add to my collection, and I asked him if he had any nervous habits. Eventually, I went upstairs and tried to find something to organize, but everything was already where it should be. I read for awhile, arranged my clothes according to color in my closet, and even moved my books on the shelf into sectioned categories.

When there was nothing left to do, I gave in. I went into the bathroom and cocooned myself in the tub, rocking back and forth, refusing to look at the empty windowsill where my ducks used to be.

If I didn't look, maybe it wouldn't feel like they were gone.

Random Fact: The heart symbol was first used for love in 1250. Before that, it represented foliage.

I leaf you.

CHAPTER TWENTY-EIGHT

The following Monday, we were all shocked when the doctor said Chad was doing so well, he could live at home now and just come into a nearby clinic for treatment sessions. I saw this look of terror cross his mother's face, then she asked the doctor about a zillion questions on how to take care of him and what to do if something went wrong. He reassured her, and then reassured her some more. He said that typically leukemia patients got to go home after the first round of treatments, but Chad had to stay in longer because of the infections. Now that he was stable in that regard, he should be at home where he could sleep better at night, "without nurses coming in to check his vitals every two hours."

Chad gave him a thumbs up for that. It was a whirlwind of a day. The doctor had mentioned maybe releasing Chad before, but none of us had believed it enough to do anything in preparation. We bounced off each trying to gather weeks worth of accumulated cards and gifts and Chad's socks, which had migrated from his feet to very unusual places throughout the room. "I can't believe it," Mrs. Carlson kept saying. "My baby boy is coming home."

The nurse pushed Chad in a wheelchair to the car because it was "standard operating procedure," and we all followed like ducks in a row, our arms full of stuff, our hearts full of joy. Okay, so that was a cheesy Hallmark card kind of thing to say, but it was true. Chad coming home was good, really good. I drove behind Mr. Carlson's car to Chad's house. Tasha drove behind me. She'd never been to his house before. Chad's parents each got on one side of him and, since he didn't want to be helped, they hovered close enough to catch him if he fell over or slipped on the stairs to the front door.

"Come on inside," I told Tasha.

She hesitated at the bottom of the steps. "Are you sure?"

It may seem odd, me inviting someone into a house that wasn't mine, but I'd been coming to Chad's house for so many years, I often forgot I wasn't technically part of the family. "At least come in long enough to put his books down."

She looked at the pile of textbooks in her hands. "Oh, right."

Chad's mom was finding blankets and piling them in a stack on the couch. "In case you get cold," she told him.

Chad walked slowly across the living room and sunk into the big brown recliner with what could only be called a moan of pleasure. "It's good to be home," he said.

"You up for pizza?" Cameron asked. "I'll order some. Any toppings you want. And I'll get them to add one of those lava cake things."

Cameron was grinning. It was so good to see, it almost hurt. Chad's parents were smiling too, and Tasha beamed. It felt like a gift, getting to share this moment. We all stood silent for a minute or two, soaking in the feeling that maybe Chad really could beat leukemia, that he really could get better.

Chad grabbed one of the blankets and curled around it like it was a stuffed animal. "Pizza and lava cake sounds awesome. And a movie. And a video game. And..."

We all waited for him to finish, but his eyes closed and soon he was snoring softly. "That was a lot of activity today," Mr. Carlson said. "Must have worn him out."

Mrs. Carlson brushed her hand across his forehead, as she used to do when his hair would fall down over his eyes. She bent to kiss his head. "It's so good to have you home, honey," she whispered, then she looked up at the ceiling with tears in her eyes. "Thank You, God."

"I'll go get a movie and the pizza," Cameron said. His gaze found mine and I got a little limp in the knees. "Want to ride with me?"

Should I? Chad was out and probably would be until Cameron got back. I had no excuse, except that I was terrified of being alone with him. There was no doubt I would say something stupid, or do something embarrassing. "What about Tasha?" I asked. If she came with us, she could talk the whole time and there'd be less chance of me making a dork of myself.

Tasha was watching Chad. "I think I'll stay here." She quickly looked at Chad's parents. "I mean, if that's okay. I can go if you want just family here. I'd totally understand if—"

"We'd love to have you stay." Mrs. Carlson was so good at putting people at ease. I hoped to learn that quality, preferably before I got old and senile and couldn't remember what it was for. "This is a very special night for Chad and us, and it's a pleasure to have Chad's special friends here too."

Tasha's cheeks turned a pretty shade of pink. I, on the other hand, probably looked all blotchy red because I'd just realized Cameron was still looking at me, waiting for my answer.

"Okay?" I said, the word coming out more like a question.

He smiled. "Okay?"

I bit my lip. "Okay."

He chuckled. "Let's continue this fascinating conversation in the car. Since Chad's asleep, I'll let you pick the pizza toppings."

"I like anchovies."

His face scrunched up. "Really?"

"No, not really. It's just fun watching you make faces."

"On second thought, we'll just get pepperoni."

It felt good to laugh. Cameron started his car and we rode in silence, a nice silence, for awhile. At the red light before the pizza place, he glanced across at me and said, "I'm scared."

"You?" I was surprised. "Of what?"

The light turned green and he turned his attention back to the road. "Of Chad being home. At the hospital, you know people are there who can help if he gets sick or has a reaction or something. Mom's going to stay home with Chad during the day, but what if they leave me to watch him when they go to the grocery store or stuff, and something terrible happens?"

I didn't know what to say so didn't say anything.

"It's awesome that he's home," he continued. "I'm really, really glad he's home. I'm just nervous. I'd feel better if there was a nurse staying with us."

We pulled into the pizza drive through and Cameron ordered three medium pepperoni pizzas plus a lava cake, then he drove to the video store. He put the car in park and rubbed his hand over his head. The tuft over his left ear went upright. "Why do I do that?"

"What? Make your hair stick out?"

He looked at me and shook his head. "Why do I tell you all the stupid things I'm thinking? It's like whatever is not cool about me comes out whenever I'm around you."

I'm sure I was making a face at that point. "You should hear the things the kids at the freak table tell me."

"You've gotten to be kind of inspiring, haven't you?"

"Me?" I laughed. "Inspiring?"

"I've heard about your table. How kids who used to sit by themselves all sit together now. And they're okay with who they are, instead of trying to fake being what they're not to impress other kids. I'm impressed."

"Don't be impressed with me," I said, getting out of the car and heading for the store. "It just happened."

"Nothing just happens, Victoria." He held open the door for me and I felt gangly and uncoordinated, a feeling which came to fruition when I tripped over the carpet and almost fell at Cameron's feet. He caught my arm but then let go quick. "And I've been impressed with you for a long time."

He wandered off to look at movies and I floated in the other direction, going down the aisle pretending to look but not seeing a thing. Had he really said that? To me? Was I having an asthma attack? I didn't have asthma, but maybe I was developing it. I couldn't seem to breath all of a sudden.

"I didn't know you liked horror movies."

My eyes focused on Cameron, then on the row of movies in front of me. "I hate horror movies."

"You know, you're not being much help to me making decisions tonight."

"I didn't know you asked me along to be helpful."

He smiled and his eyes did some kind of twinkle thing. "I didn't."

I grinned like a ninny. "Well, then, let's get your movie and pick up your pizzas before we end up with a horror film and anchovies to ruin the evening."

He held the door open again for me on the way out, but this time I didn't trip. "You are a very unusual girl, Victoria."

I climbed into his car. "The correct word is abnormal."

"Unique. Intriguingly different. There are lots of ways to say it that are positive."

Abnormal and positive: two words not often connected with each other. I thought of Shane, and Kendra, and all the other kids I'd met lately who were great in their own ways.

There were real possibilities here. Here as in me not thinking so badly of myself, as well as here in Cameron's car.

It was a perfect evening. Chad woke up and ate two pieces of pizza, and Cameron's funny movie revealed that if Tasha laughs hard, she snorts, which makes her super embarrassed, so then she talks and talks. It was hilarious. Chad kept us all up late telling jokes just to get her to snort again.

I didn't get home until midnight, and even at that, I didn't go to sleep for a long time. Possibilities were a strange new thing to me and kept me awake with their whispers of hope.

I wasn't sure if my heart could handle all the stuff going on in my head.

Random Fact: If you turn your underwear inside out and put them on, the whole universe is wearing your underwear except for you.

That's not really a fact, but it's funny, so I'm keeping it.

CHAPTER TWENTY-NINE

Tasha avoided the freak table Monday and Tuesday of the following week. I figured she was either embarrassed about movie night and was avoiding me, or she was overwhelmed with the assortment of insecure people at our table now, and how openly we talked about our oddities. My guess was the latter. After a lifetime of trying to cover over and hide mine, I was loving it, but Tasha was closer to normal than the rest of us so maybe it was too much for her.

This is why it surprised me when she appeared that Wednesday at lunch, tray in hand, tears in her eyes.

"I have to talk to you, Vicky," she gasped out, like she'd run a lap around the building before getting her food. "The Bible says if someone has wronged you, you're supposed to go talk to them about it in person, and if you've wronged someone else, you're supposed to go talk with them, but I didn't want to talk to you about it because I feel terrible and have tried to not feel the way I do but it hasn't stopped it and I know it's the right thing to do to tell you but I thought maybe if I didn't say anything it would all work out but it hasn't worked out and it hasn't gone away and, oh goodness, you know I talk too much when I get nervous. I'm sorry."

She sure could use a lot of words to say nothing at all. "What are you talking about?" I asked.

Tasha set her tray down with a thud. "I've fallen in love with your boyfriend."

She shouldn't have said that just as I was taking a drink. I spit apple juice all over my lunch and a section of the surrounding table. The grossness was accentuated by every kid at the table leaning back and saying, "Ew!" in unison. Emily, a newer girl to our group who had OCD, attacked the table with antibacterial wipes while I wiped my mouth and said, "He's not my boyfriend."

"But you spend all your time together. Everybody thinks he is." She pulled on her fingers and stared at her plate. Was she checking to see if I'd spit on her food?

"We don't spend any time together," I argued. "Except last weekend. Normally, he doesn't even talk to me, and I—Wait. Who are you talking about?"

She flapped her eyelashes at me. "Chad, of course."

"Chad?" I almost shouted.

"Shhh!" She sat down across from me and whispered, "Do you want everybody in school to know?"

"Know what?"

"That I'm a terrible friend." She was on the verge of tears. "I didn't mean for this to happen. Back when he got diagnosed, a bunch of us from the youth group decided to visit Chad because it's what Jesus would do, but then he was so nice and you were so nice and I just kept coming back, and then he wanted to study the Bible together and then you would disappear and I just found myself wanting to be with him every chance I could, and..." She dropped her head onto her hand. "I don't know how I'm going to tell Chad I can't come and see him anymore without telling him why, but I just can't tell him why."

I was swimming in a pool of vague, murky information.

"Wait, wait," I said, my hand out in plea. "I am totally confused here."

Kendra had sidled up to Tasha. "This is like a soap opera. I can picture the scene in the hospital, you telling Chad you can't see him anymore, your heart breaking, and him—"

"He's not in the hospital now. He goes to a clinic for treatments." That was a useless bit of information considering the moment, but it was all I could come up with.

"Well, you should—"

The squeal of the school loudspeaker caught our attention, and then the school secretary's voice filled the room. "Victoria Dane. Victoria Dane. Please come to Mr. Seecord's office immediately."

Everyone stared at me. "What did you do?" Shane asked. "I've never heard them call a student out of lunch before."

"I don't know."

Uncomfortable does not describe how I felt, packing up my lunch and crossing the now silent cafeteria while the entire world—or so it seemed—stared me down. I sang "four little ducks went out to play" in my head out the cafeteria and down the hall. At the open door of Mr. Seecord's office I paused. He stood with his back to me, a paper in his hand. He turned and I took a step back. His gaze looked disappointed, though I could not fathom why, and behind the disappointment was...fear?

"Is it Chad?" My throat closed up and I could feel my fingernails digging into my palm. "Has something happened?"

"Sit down, Victoria."

It had to be about Chad. I caught myself praying for strength to not fall apart. Strange, how you can think God isn't real all day long, but when the world caves in, you still find yourself asking for His help. I fell into the chair facing Mr. Seecord's desk and my lunch bag dropped to the floor, forgotten. I couldn't imagine ever eating again. Why wasn't he saying something? Why was he just looking at me, searching my eyes like that?

Mr. Seecord held up the paper in his hand. "Who did you tell about the bomb threat?"

"What?" My mind was like a computer when it freezes up and nothing works, not even the mouse, and you have to shut it down and restart it to get it going again. I shook my head. "Didn't you call me here to tell me something terrible about Chad?"

"Chad is fine as far as I know. I called you here to ask you about this." He handed the paper over but I could not see what it said. My relief about Chad was so great I was crying, right there in his office, and I didn't even care.

He handed me a tissue and waited for me to blow my nose and wipe my eyes. I finally picked up the paper and looked it over. It didn't say much, just one line. "It's still there," I read aloud, then looked at Mr. Seecord. "What's still there?"

With his one arm angled on the desk, he leaned toward me. "Victoria, I need you to be honest with me. Totally honest. Did you or Chad tell anyone about Keith's bomb threat?"

That's what this is all about? "No. I haven't said a word to anyone but Chad, and he promised he wouldn't tell anyone either."

"You're sure he wouldn't slip?"

"He's never broken a promise to me. Ever." I handed the paper back with a question. "Where did this come from?"

His scowl was a bit frightening. Whatever this message meant, he was taking it seriously. "I got it in the mail. There's no return address, but I traced it to the town where Keith is incarcerated."

"Do you think it's from him?" The words started to compute and I gasped. "You think he's saying there really is a bomb here?"

"It could be a prank. Maybe somebody who was in juvenile detention talked to Keith, and then got released and thought it would be funny to scare us."

"I don't think it's funny at all."

He frowned. "Neither do I." He stood. "You're sure you didn't tell anyone?"

"I'm sure. It's not the kind of the thing you mention on accident."

With a nod, he motioned that I could go, telling me firmly I was not to talk to anyone but Chad about any of this. I turned to leave, but had no desire to return to the cafeteria. Everyone would want to know what I'd been called for, and I wasn't any good at making stuff up. I'd get my coat out of my locker and finish my lunch on the bench outside. Some cold air might clear my head.

"Mr. Seecord?" I asked before I left, pointing at the paper. "What will you do?"

He folded the paper and put it in his pocket. His voice sounded like he was gearing up for war. "I'm going to call the police, and then I'm driving out to the detention center to have a talk with Keith Childers."

Random Fact: In medical dramas, about 66% of patients who are administered CPR survive long enough to be discharged from the hospital. In reality, depending on the circumstances, CPR has a success rate between 2% and 18%.

Reality stinks sometimes.

CHAPTER THIRTY

I'd left my lunch in Mr. Seecord's office, so I spent the rest of the lunch period wandering around the school building, an ignorant version of Nancy Drew, wondering how a person could hide a bomb so well two days of police searching couldn't find it. The logical side of my brain said there wasn't one, that Keith was just trying to keep us all in a state of fear. The other side of my brain insisted logic had nothing to do with a lot of things that happened in life, which brought my thoughts to Tasha. And Chad.

I didn't see Tasha the rest of the day, and when I got to the clinic after school, it was no surprise she was not there. Chad was in the recliner, a wet washcloth over his eyes. Alecia would make some crack about it being a new fashion statement, but I wasn't in the mood to try to be funny. Chad getting out of the hospital had been great, but it made some things harder. Like chemo day. His mom would bring him into the clinic for a morning treatment, but there'd be delays or they'd have to check blood work first, and hours would go by while he waited to be shot up with stuff that made him miserable. Not to mention the miserable part.

"Hey," I said, warning him of my arrival since he couldn't see. "The washcloth is new. What's with your eyes?"

"They're giving me arsenic," he growled.

I gulped. "Like as in the poison?"

"Yeah. For some reason my body doesn't like being poisoned. I'd throw up if it didn't hurt everywhere to move."

Since he couldn't see the concern on my face, I came close and very gently put my hand on his shoulder. I'd been forcing myself to touch someone once a day, usually Alex because he'd pull away instead of wanting to hug me like Mom did. The more I practiced, the easier it got, like taking one toy car out of the row. I let my hand rest there and said, "That's terrible. Can I do anything?"

"Could you get me a new pair of eyes?" He pulled off the washcloth and I gasped out loud. His eyes were blood red and swollen. How was it possible that anything doing that to the human body could be good?

"Excuse me." A nurse came in and we shuffled around so she could get to Chad's arm to take his blood pressure. "He's having a reaction," she said.

"I noticed." I restrained myself from asking what they were going to do about it, and why they didn't stop the pain. The medical team was doing everything they could. Cancer just stunk. The way to fight it stunk. It wasn't their fault.

"You might want to sit over there." She nodded her chin to a chair several feet away. "We'll be checking his blood pressure every five minutes, and keeping him under observation until we can get this reaction under control. You can stay, but you'll need to keep out of the way."

"Okay." I patted Chad's shoulder once before I went to the chair. "If they aren't rushing you to the hospital ICU, that means it's not as terrible as it looks, right?"

"Oh, it's terrible," Chad said with a groan. He'd stopped holding those back when I was around. With his mom, he still tried to act like it wasn't so bad. "It's just not dangerous. There's a difference."

"Yeah." I waited until the nurse left, then told him about Mr. Seecord and the letter. It was good to have something to get his mind off the pain, even if it was a creepy, potentially violent mystery. We quieted down when the nurse came back five minutes later. I wanted to ask if it would help if I rubbed his feet or something, but for one, I'd rub feet probably as well as a block of wood, and for another, the nurse had told me to stay out of the way.

I searched for another interesting topic. "Is Tasha coming to study with you later?" Chad's mom had hired a tutor to help keep Chad up on his schoolwork during the non-chemo days. Those evenings, Tasha would come over and they'd study the Bible together.

"She won't be coming anymore. She called me after school, right before you got here."

"Did she say why?"

"No. I asked her and she said a lot of stuff, she even started crying, but none of it made any sense."

I saw a muscle in his jaw tighten. Did he have feelings for Tasha? "Maybe it's just temporary."

"I guess she's another one of those crisis friends, who just lasted longer than most."

"Crisis friends?" I'd never heard that phrase before. He shifted in his chair but moaned at the movement. I wished for the hundredth time to have access to something that would take away the pain. How did he endure it over and over again?

"If I was into keeping notebooks like you," he said, "I'd make one of the different kinds of friends you get when you have cancer." He draped the washcloth over his eyes again. "I'd start with the patient's former friends, who all have to decide if they will remain your friends or not. Those who were friends because you were fun go first, because cancer is not fun. Those who were friends because you did things for them disappear next, because when you're puking and losing your hair you can't do much for others. Those who were friends because they like you in general stick it out longer in hopes that you will return to your likeable self."

I wondered if he was thinking of Alecia and Dan, and which category he would put them in. "Then there are the friends," I put in, "who will stick with you through the puke, without your hair, and be by your side until you beat the cancer."

"Or it beats me."

Even though I knew he needed me to say it—especially on a day like today—it still hurt coming out of my mouth. "Yes, or until it beats you."

He sighed. "A lot of people don't have that kind. I'm glad I do."

I was getting teary and that wouldn't do. "And you don't think Tasha is that kind?"

"Can't get ahead of ourselves," he said. "Next there would be family friends, the people who have no choice but to remain in connection with you because they are related. They start out very involved and spend lots of time cheering you up, until it drags on and on and they run out of ideas. Then they drift off, or start calling your parents for updates so they don't have to actually talk to you."

"It would help if you weren't so insightful," I said.

The nurse came back and checked his blood pressure again.

"And then are people like Tasha, who weren't friends before, but they're drawn to people who are suffering. Those are the empathetic souls who feel good nurturing people in need."

I frowned. "You're starting to sound cynical."

"My eyeballs are popping out of my head. Give me a break." He felt around for his cup of water and took a sip.

"The church people have actually been great, maybe because they're doing it for God instead of for me, so it doesn't matter that I'm not always perky and appreciative. But with Tasha, I thought maybe it was more..."

I sat forward. "More what?"

"More than just because she loved God. Like maybe—maybe she—"

"Maybe she was falling for you?"

He shook his head and then clutched his stomach. "Not much chance of that. I mean, look at me. If I ever was attractive, I'm not now. I don't blame her for getting lost. I just—"

The nurse would have to push me out of the way next time she came. I walked over to Chad's chair and put my hand back on his shoulder. Then I leaned down and said softly, "She thinks you're my boyfriend."

"You're boyfriend?" Chad laughed out loud. "Victoria Dane—my girlfriend. Imagine that."

He said it plenty loud, and at just the wrong time. A nurse didn't come in just as he was saying I was his girlfriend, but Cameron did. He took one look at the two of us, close together, my hand on his shoulder, and backed out of the room without a word.

Random Fact: In Ancient Greece, to declare your love for someone, you threw an apple at them.

If you want to throw love-declaring food at me, throw chocolate.

CHAPTER THIRTY-ONE

It's not like I could just call Cameron up and say, "I'm not Chad's girlfriend, by the way, in case you might by chance be a little bit interested in me." With Chad in the clinic most afternoons, I didn't even have an excuse to go to his house, where I might accidentally run into Cameron and be able to tell him a funny story about Tasha thinking I was Chad's girlfriend.

I tried to block it from my mind and focus on school and homework and I even spent some time thinking about Mr. Seecord's essay, though all that did was make me feel worse. Mr. Seecord himself looked pretty bummed during history class, so when lunch period rolled around, I bypassed the cafeteria and went to see him instead. With a look down the hall in both directions to make sure no one was within earshot, I went inside his room and asked, "Were you able to see Keith? Did he confess to writing the letter?"

Mr. Seecord was standing at the board. The piece of chalk broke in his hand. He threw the two pieces away, then turned to me. "They wouldn't let me see him. I should have remembered that only parents or guardians are allowed."

"Were you able to—"

"It was a dead end, Victoria." He'd never cut me off before. The way he stared at the chalkboard with his one fist clenched tight made me think he wanted to run his fingernails down it just out of frustration. Did something else happen while he was there? Maybe he toured the grounds and saw Keith outside, and maybe Keith did some signal or yelled something and...

I needed to reign in my imagination and stick with the facts. "So you don't know if he sent the letter or not?"

"I don't know anything. And I don't like it." He got a fresh piece of chalk out of a little box on his desk. Mr. Seecord never used broken pieces of chalk. Said life was too short to endure that kind of stress. I never was able to tell if he was joking or if half pieces of chalk really did annoy him that much. "You'd better get to lunch."

I recognized a dismissal when I heard one. It wouldn't do any good to ask more questions, so I made my way out of the classroom and on to the cafeteria. Right away, I noticed Tasha was not at our table. I scanned the room and found her sitting with some of the kids from her church youth group. I might not be able to fix the mess with Cameron, but I could at least try to fix the one with her.

"Tasha," I said, approaching from behind. "Can I talk to you a minute?"

She did not turn, but stopped eating and started pulling on her fingers. "Sure." She excused herself from the table and left her tray. I led the way to the one empty table left in the cafeteria and set my lunch down. She sat across from me, her eyes worried, her bottom lip between her teeth.

"I'm not Chad's girlfriend," I said right away. "I never was. He's the best friend in the world, and I think he's awesome, but I don't feel that way about him."

Tasha sniffed and wiped her nose. "You're just trying to make me feel better."

"Trust me," I said, biting my cheek, then thinking of Chad. "I'm not creative enough for that. If you promise not to tell anyone..."

She tilted her head and nodded, her face showing me she expected to hear something dreadful, like I was secretly engaged to Chad and we didn't want anyone to know. "I like his brother."

Her eyes went wide. "What?"

"Cameron. His older brother." I was going to bite a hole in my cheek. I tried chewing on my hair like Kendra. Yuck. "I've had a crush on him for years. But don't tell him."

"Really?" Tasha's face flushed and her eyes brightened. She really was very pretty to look at. Why wouldn't Chad like her? "You mean it?"

"Yeah." At least me liking Cameron did her some good. As far as my life went, it was making things far too complicated.

"So you don't mind me spending time with Chad?"

Now that was a different question. I didn't mind her liking him, but was I okay with her being with him, and the time that took away from me? "Well, I guess if you end up spending every waking moment together, maybe it will force me to get a life, like Alecia says."

"You? You're sacrificing your time to hang out with a friend who has cancer, and she thinks you need to get a life? I'd say it's the other way around."

"She thinks I'm codependent."

Tasha snorted, then turned red. "Well, I think you're fantastic." She looked back at her original table. "I wished I'd brought my lunch. I'm hungry."

I hadn't touched mine yet. "Why don't you go grab it? We've got five minutes left."

She came back with her tray and said a quick silent prayer before scarfing down her piece of fried chicken and a blob of what might be creamed corn. I started in on my wheat sandwich and she said between bites, "If you did want to 'get a life' though, do some things outside of the hospital and clinic and all that, what would you do?"

It was a strange thought. If I didn't spend so much time with Chad, now that the four dorks were no longer my world, what would I put in their place? Who was I without them? I had thought to wonder that about Chad, but not about myself. "Maybe I'd get a job and start saving money for college."

"That would be prudent, but not very fun. What would you do for fun? What do you like?"

What did I like? "I like putting toy cars in a row with Cameron," I said, then blushed when she grinned.

"Okay, what else?"

"What else? I think..." It felt like I was opening a door to part of my mind that had been shut up and ignored, like an old, dusty attic. "I think I'd like to try out for track. I like to run. It clears my head and there's a rhythm to it that's very orderly."

"Interesting." She wolfed down her last bites just as the bell rang. "I wouldn't have guessed that about you."

"Me neither." I tossed my paper bag in the trash on our way out of the cafeteria.

"Funny how we can surprise ourselves sometimes," Tasha said in the hallway. She opened her locker and put away three books and got out two different ones. "I was surprised when I realized I cared about Chad."

"You should go see him after school." I slung my backpack over my shoulder. Someday doctors would discover that kids carrying twenty pounds of books on their backs for four years was detrimental to the spine.

"But that's your time."

"I'll let you have it today." I smiled. "But don't make a habit of it."

She squealed and hugged me and I tried not to stiffen. It wasn't too bad, since most of what she hugged was my backpack. "You're the best," she said, and flittered off to class like a girl in love.

I watched her go, hoping I had done the right thing. If Chad didn't like her, I'd just added to the mess his life was right now. But I was taking the chance that he did, and besides, I wanted to use that time for something else. Nothing that Alecia would count as getting a life, but for me, it was yet another step that would take courage I wasn't sure I had.

Random Fact: The average human accidentally eats 8 spiders in their life.

Do those numbers go up if you eat cafeteria lunches?

CHAPTER THIRTY-TWO

As soon as I got home from school, I got online and pulled up a search engine. I had just found the site for the closest juvenile detention center when Mom and Alex came through the front door.

"Victoria, you're home!" Mom got the milk out of the refrigerator. She'd always been a milk-and-cookies-after-school kind of mom, which was great. "What a pleasant surprise. Want a cookie?"

"In just a minute," I called out, writing the number and shutting the computer down. "I need to make a phone call."

I closed myself in my room and dialed the number, rocking back and forth just a little as I waited for someone to answer. A gruff voice came over the line and I imagined a jail warden with weight-lifter shoulders and a long, scruffy beard. "Um..." I said.

"Can I help you?" the man repeated.

"Yes, I mean, I hope so." I stopped rocking and tugged on my hair. "I'm a classmate of Keith Childers. I was wondering how long he was—um—incarcerated for?"

"I'm afraid I can't give out that information, ma'am."

"You can't tell me when he's getting out?"

"I can only share that with parents or guardians."

Not helpful. "So if he got out, like, tomorrow, nobody would know about it?"

"Nobody except the people picking him up."

"So he could be out right now?"

"As I said, I can't share that information."

"Do you know what cult he got involved in?"

"Couldn't tell you that even if I knew."

I said something polite and hung up. I trudged down the stairs and Mom asked me what was wrong. "I just made the most unhelpful phone call of my life."

She handed me a cookie. Even though I was past the days when a cookie solved problems, they still tasted good. "Want to tell me about it?" she asked.

Mom had her masters in counseling. She was the person who showed up during crisis situations and gave people a shoulder to cry on. Sometimes I wondered if I was adopted. How could she have birthed a child who hid in the bathtub?

She sat across from me and waited, like a good counselor would. Next to her, Alex worked on his second cookie and gulped down his glass of milk. "Slow down, sweetie," Mom told him. "There's not a fire."

When he finished, she sent him to the living room to do his homework and focused again on me. I always appreciated that, how she made it clear she wanted to know what I had to say. "I called the juvenile detention center."

She sat back a little. "That's...unexpected." She picked up a cookie and nibbled on it. "Why did you call them?"

"To ask about Keith."

Concern lined her forehead. "Why?"

"Well..." I didn't want to tell her about the bomb, even if I had been free to. "It's been about a year now. I don't know how long he was sentenced for, but you know, sometimes people get out early on good behavior or whatever. I wanted to ask when he was getting out."

"And did they tell you?"

"No," I mumbled. "They wouldn't tell me anything. What if he was only sentenced for one year? What if he shows up at our school next week?"

With one fingernail, Mom dug a chocolate chip out of the cookie and slipped it into her mouth. "Well, I don't know how long he's in for, but I do know you don't need to worry about him coming back to your school."

I watched her pick out another chocolate chip. Was that a nervous habit, or she just didn't want to waste calories on anything that wasn't chocolate? "Why not?" Just the thought of seeing him again made me want to run to the bathtub. I pulled on my hair. I needed to grow my hair out if I was going to keep up that habit.

"After it happened..." Mom was good at talking vague about difficult things. "I spent a good bit of time talking with the principal, and the school asked me to talk with Keith's family. I went over to their house several times. His parents are split up and he lives with his mom and her boyfriend." She frowned and looked her cookie over, then set it back on the plate, an uncharacteristic move for her. I took the cookie to eat it while she talked, so she wouldn't be disgusted later to see that someone had eaten off one and then put it back. "It is not a good home situation," she said. "I wouldn't be surprised if drugs are part of their lives." She sighed and shook her head, looking at the table as if wondering where her cookie had gone. "Which is such a psychological danger in itself, but even more so when someone's on anti-depressants or other emotion-altering drugs like Ke—" She glanced at me and her face filled with the same guilty look Alex got when he snuck an extra cookie without permission. "You don't need to hear all of that. I will tell you, though, that the principal assured me Keith would never be allowed back into your school, and his mother told me that once he got out, they were moving away and starting over again."

142

I handed the rest of Mom's cookie back to her. "Really? That's good news."

"Glad I could help." She smiled and took a bite. "Now fill me in on you."

I gave her an update on Chad, and then on me, and for the first time felt like we were talking more like two women friends than a kid giving a rundown on her day to a parent. I told her about giving away my ducks and her eyes glistened.

"Victoria, I'm so proud of you," she said. She reached across and touched my hand and I didn't pull away.

"What do you think about me trying out for the track team?" I asked.

"Track?" She cocked her head to the side. "What has happened to my girl?"

I shrugged but smiled. "I'm not sure, but I think it might be a good thing."

She wiped her eyes. "I think so too." Then she grinned. "Now, you told me about Tasha liking Chad. Do you want to finally admit how you feel about his big brother?"

Random Fact: Charlie Chaplin once entered a Charlie Chaplin look-alike contest. He won third place.

Alex would quote Mater from Cars and say, "That's funny right there."

CHAPTER THIRTY-THREE

Mom and I sat at the kitchen table all afternoon and talked about my love life. Or my non-love life. It felt good to finally get it all out, and when I told her about the mess I was in, she gave some helpful advice, though once again, following it meant putting myself in a situation where I needed more courage than I had. When had life gotten so scary? At least my fear of Keith coming back to school was gone. I would have to tell Mr. Seecord what Mom said about them moving away once he got out. What a relief.

In the meantime, though, I needed to drop by the clinic. It was after supper, and Chad and Tasha would probably be finishing up their Bible study. Mom said I should offer to drive him home, and then when I got to his house, just talk to Cameron and explain. It sounded so simple when she said it, but I was tied up in knots before I even got in the car. I didn't know what I would say, or how I would start, but it turned out to not matter anyway because when I got to the clinic, Tasha was gone and Cameron was there.

"Oh, I'm sorry." I had barged into the room like usual, but as soon as I saw Cameron, I started backing away. I'm sure that didn't look good, but I wasn't prepared for him to be there, and my brain sort of short-circuited. "I'll come back later."

"No, it's okay." His voice was curt. He stood and made his way toward the door. "I'll go to the waiting room and you two can be alone."

"Alone?" I didn't want to be alone with Chad. Oh brother. Cameron tried to get out the door but I was in the way. I stepped to my left, but he stepped to his right, so we both stepped to the other side, then we both went back to the middle.

"You guys look like you're doing some weird line dance," Chad said from his bed. Cameron grunted and put his hands on my shoulders. I was so surprised I went completely still and he was able to get around me.

I wanted to tell him not to go, but just as I opened my mouth, a nurse came in the door and crashed into Cameron. "Sorry," she said. Now his hands were on her shoulders to keep her from falling over. Normally, when I saw someone touching someone else, I was glad it wasn't me, but not this time. "I heard Chad's having some new symptoms." She made her way around Cameron and asked Chad, "What are you hearing?"

Chad sat up a little. "This high pitched noise, like my ears are ringing, but really loud." He rubbed his forehead. "And I'm seeing black spots whenever I look to the side."

"Which side?"

"Both sides."

"Hmm, let me..." She looked over at us. "Would you two mind taking a break to the waiting room or the snack room for a bit? I want to check on a couple of things with Chad. We need to find out if these new things are from his meds or something else."

"Uh, okay." I turned and ran into Cameron, who had not moved. It was far from a romantic moment, since he was frowning down at me. I waved at Chad, then Cameron and I left the room and walked down the hall through the maze of doorways and corridors toward the snack room. The clinic wasn't as big as the hospital, so didn't have a full cafeteria. I ordered a latte and Cameron got a bagel. I felt ridiculously nervous, especially since he wouldn't stop frowning. This was not how I'd planned it, not what Mom had said to do, and I was not good at adapting when plans changed.

I bit my cheek and since it was already sore, pulled on my hair instead, but that felt too girly. I fidgeted as he sat at a table and methodically cut his bagel in half and smeared cream cheese on it. I took a sip of my latte and then reached down in my bag for my notebook.

"Did you know that bagel-related injuries are so common that hospitals have a special name for them?"

He directed his frown from the bagel to me. "What?"

I opened my notebook of random facts and read number forty-seven. "Bagel-related injuries, BRIs, send as many as two thousand Americans to the hospital annually," I read. "I think those are mostly from people trying to cut them in half and cutting their hands." I gestured toward his bagel. "It's a good thing you used a plastic knife."

"Well, if I'd cut myself, where better to be than in a clinic?"

I smiled and he smiled but then he frowned again, like smiling was against the rules when he was with me. I swallowed and tried to put my plan into this new setting. "Can I tell you a story?"

His lips dropped lower. "You don't need to entertain me, Victoria. Chad will probably be busy with the nurse all evening. You can go home."

"I don't want to go home. I want to tell you a story."

He took a bite of bagel and made me wait while he chewed and swallowed. "Why?"

"Why what?"

"Why do you want to tell me a story?"

"Because of what happened the other day, and—"

"What if I don't want to listen?"

Why was he making this so hard? "You should let a person answer if you ask them a question." Now I was frowning too. "And even if you don't want to listen, I would think that, as my friend, you would—"

Cameron stood. He gathered his bagel, plastic knife, and cream cheese container and threw them all in the nearest trash can. He'd only taken one bite. Then he came back and stood next to the table where I still sat. "I don't want to be your friend, Vicky. It's too hard. I'm sorry."

He walked away. I sat at the table with my latte and my notebook of useless, random facts, watching him go and trying not to cry. I'd have to tell Mom that even plans to share your heart can go awry if the other person can't stand you.

Random Fact: A Ten Gallon Hat will only hold 3/4 of a gallon.

Life's full of false promises.

CHAPTER THIRTY-FOUR

Tasha floated on air the next day while I lived under a thundercloud. She didn't seem to notice my grey mood and gushed about how much fun she'd had with Chad the afternoon before and how his eyes had lit up when she came and surprised him at the clinic, and how she thought that maybe, just maybe, he liked her too.

All we needed was music and the scene could have turned into a song and dance routine like in a musical.

"I'm happy for you," I groused, and somewhere deep down, I really was. Sure, she was taking away my best friend. Sure, the guy I had fallen for didn't want to spend even five minutes in my company. But what did I have to complain about, really? I didn't have cancer.

"Did you know our youth group is planning a big barbeque dinner and bake sale for a fundraiser for Chad's family?" Tasha ate a lot when she was excited. And fast. Kendra with her ADHD couldn't even keep up with her today. "I can't wait. It's next week. I've been helping, and the nurses said Chad should be able to come for at least some of it. I think it's going to be a great success. We're even going to sell those rubber bracelets that say, 'Fight for a cure.'"

"Yeah, a bunch of people wearing bracelets will make a big difference," I grumbled.

She came down to earth for a second. "Every little bit counts, doesn't it?"

"Yes, it does. Sorry. I'm just being a jerk today." I needed to get over myself. If Cameron didn't want to have anything to do with me, I should just accept that and move on. I should not leave school in tears and spend a week in my bathtub, and I should definitely not buy two new ducks and mark them with my name and Cameron's name and put them on the windowsill to dream of what would never be. I should not mope around and dig chocolate chips out of all the cookies in the kitchen, or watch romantic comedies with a bowl of ice cream and a box of Kleenex so I could cry at my loveless fate.

Tasha interrupted my thoughts. "Are you going to see Chad after school today?"

I could tell she was too nice to ask that I wouldn't so she could go be with him instead. Part of me wanted to tell her to go ahead and I'd go home, but then again, if I went home I might end up following one of my whims and that wouldn't take me anyplace good. "Let's go together," I said. "I have some questions for him."

And I did. Ever since I realized I had some interests I'd never thought to pursue, I'd been wondering if Chad did too. Alecia and Dan had been able to chase their individual interests, but Chad was stuck in the cancer world for now. I was curious to know who he wanted to be, what he wanted to do, when he got out.

I made Tasha go into the room first when we got to the clinic that afternoon, just in case Cameron was there. It was a dumb thing to do, since if he was in there, he'd have to come through the door to leave and would see me hiding in the hallway. But you do dumb things when your heart is involved, and my heart wanted to stay as far away from Cameron Carlson as possible.

"Come on in, Vicky," she called.

I walked inside where Chad was sitting up in his recliner. His eyes looked good. "Are the black spots gone?"

"They're worse." He shifted in his chair. "But since my second round of chemo is up in ten days, we—as in they—decided to see if I can wait it out."

Tasha pulled up a chair to sit close. "Does it hurt?"

"No." He smiled at her and I tried to discern if his smile for her was special, different than the way he smiled at me. I couldn't quite tell, but Tasha melted into her chair, so she apparently thought so. "But seeing big black dots whenever you move your eyes is...dark. Hopefully it will go away before my retinas disintegrate."

"That's horrible." Tasha grabbed his arm. "Don't even say that."

"Don't get me started on what the chemo might do." He laughed at the fear on her face. "Stop worrying. If I've made it through eight and a half weeks of treatment without turning green or a limb falling off, I think the last ten days should be okay."

She crossed her arms, but smiled. "You're not funny."

He grinned. "And you're not really mad."

"You're right."

Things were getting a little mushy around the edges. I was okay with Tasha liking my best friend, but not with her turning him into a sap while I was still there in the room. If Alex had been with me, he could say something blunt, like, "They're making cow eyes at each other!" which worked very effectively on couples at the mall. But as my little brother was not there, I would have to make do.

I found another chair in the hall and dragged it inside. "I have questions for you," I announced, sitting and pulling out a brand new notebook. This one had a pink cover.

"You're starting another one?" Chad shifted again. Was he in pain, or was it just an unconscious movement out of habit now? "What strange information are you collecting now?"

"I want to know about you."

"About me? What about me?"

Tasha smiled and jumped in. "When you get out. What do you want to do? Who do you want to be? What are your interests?"

He looked at her long enough for all of us to know his interest was in her. She blushed and beamed and I pretended I didn't exist for awhile until Chad finally turned to me. "I'm not answering any questions for a pink notebook."

"But pink is the color for cancer."

His mouth tipped. "For breast cancer."

Tasha turned red as a beet and I'm sure I did too. "Good point. What's the color for leukemia?"

"I don't think there is one."

Tasha started pulling on her fingers. "Don't you have another notebook, Vicky?"

"I can't write his answers in any of my other notebooks. They're for other things." She hadn't known me long enough to know that her suggestion was impossible. Some things in life were sacred.

"You don't have to write it all down, you know," Chad said, laughing. "You could just listen."

"But I might not remember everything you say," I argued, clicking my pen in a way I was sure was annoying but I couldn't seem to quit.

"Then you could ask me again."

Tasha giggled. "You two are funny." I pondered this strange comment while she asked Chad our questions.

"What's with the sudden interest in my interests?"

His question was directed at me, so I answered, "Now that we won't be doing four dorks things all the time, we can do more what we're interested in personally. I realized I want to start running. What do you want to do?"

"I want to not have cancer."

"That's a given. But then what?"

"That's about all I can think about at the moment. It's kind of my life." He let his head rest back and looked up at the trim running along the underside of the ceiling. "I never had big ambitions. I like doing what other people are doing. I like going to Dan's games because it makes him happy, and I liked helping you learn how to play with other kids. I like hanging out at the graveyard on Tuesdays and studying in my basement over pizza."

"But those are things for others," Tasha insisted. "What about you, personally?"

"I don't like making decisions, so maybe doing what other people want to do is what I want to do, because then I don't have to think about it too much."

She made a face. "That doesn't make sense."

"He's always been that way." I said. I put my pink notebook far in the back of my backpack, and my pen in the front pocket with my other writing utensils. I'd branched out lately and started putting my pens and pencils in the same section. "About a year ago, when Alecia got on a cosmetology kick, he let her style his hair and put in these terrible blond highlights."

He was smiling and it was such a nice thing to see. "That was a bad idea. They didn't wash out for months."

"I bet you looked cute."

He pointed to the windowsill. "My hair was the color of Vicks' rubber duckies. I looked like a dork."

She giggled again and asked about the ducks and we spent the afternoon telling her stories to get her to laugh and snort. I hadn't seen Chad have that much fun in a long time. Tasha was good for him. And I was happy for him. I really was. When he got out after this was all over, he'd want to spend time with her, to do whatever she liked doing.

I needed to prepare myself for a future not just without two of my three best friends, but possibly all of them.

"You know," Chad said as the nurse brought his dinner and we packed up to go. Cameron would be coming to pick him up in about half an hour and I wanted to be long gone by then. "Your questions are kind of like Mr. Seecord's question."

I didn't see the connection. "What do you mean?"

"What's worth living and dying for. It's kind of like asking, who are you? What's important to you? Because what's important to you is what you end up living and dying for, even if you don't consciously choose it."

He was talking about death again. I hefted my backpack over my shoulder, glad it was time to go. "Well..."

"Have you decided yet?" Tasha asked. She had stood but hadn't budged from the side of Chad's recliner. She had no need to be nervous about Cameron showing up, so she could dally all she wanted.

"I think so."

They must have talked about this before, when I wasn't around. Tasha sat back down. "Tell me."

"I think it's living." He waved his hand toward the bedside table. "I started to write some of the essay, but haven't gotten my thoughts in total order yet. At first all I could think about was cancer, and how cancer wasn't worth dying for. But then I realized that I'm not going through all of this for cancer. I'm going through all of this for the chance to live without cancer. It's life I'm fighting for. The chance to live is worth dying for. So life is worth living for, too. You know, really living a life that matters, not just existing or being here just because we are. Having a purpose."

"That's beautiful," Tasha said. I didn't say anything. I still didn't want to think about it.

"Like I said," he added. "I haven't figured out how to say it clearly, but I'm working on it."

Tasha reached for his hand. "I'd love to read your essay when you finish it."

He held her hand and smiled. "It'll have to wait for awhile. It's hard to write around these big black polka-dots in my eyes."

"I could help you next time I visit. You could dictate and I could write it."

"I think I'd rather just hang out with you."

She melted again and I slipped away. Strange how you can be so happy for someone else and so sad for yourself at the same time. I needed to get a new duck with Tasha's name on it and put it close to Chad on the windowsill. But even if I did that, and even if her duck stood closer to his than mine, I still wasn't taking mine down. Some things were worth keeping, and the kind of friendship Chad and I had was one of them.

Random Fact: Jedi is an official religion in Australia. It has an estimated 70,000 followers.

Unusual, they are.

CHAPTER THIRTY-FIVE

The big barbeque night was set for three days before the end of Chad's second round of treatments. After that, he got a break for a week, and then had to get checked back into the hospital for a big three week finale that would hopefully be the end. The idea was that the stuff they did would kill all the cancer cells already there and prevent new ones from coming or spreading, and though he'd do a few maintenance things over the next few years, he would be able to be as active and "normal" as he was before.

That was the idea anyway. Nobody knew if Chad's cancer would go along with the plan or not.

As it got toward the end, they did bone marrow biopsies and talked about a stem cell transplant, and of course threw around lots of numbers about his platelets and other things I tuned out. If I was a truly good friend, I would be learning all the words and their definitions and what it meant when something went high or low. Tasha had compiled a whole three-ring binder of research she'd done on leukemia. She could keep up with Chad's parents whenever they talked about the latest results or concerns. I tended to leave the room. To me, it all came down to life or death, and anytime they started in I wanted to run away. I didn't, but I wanted to.

Instead, I tried to put my mind toward something else, which was hard to do when Mr. Seecord asked every day if we were working on our essay. Seemed like every lesson he taught lately was about some historical event where people had to choose what they would live and die for. We discussed Tiananmen Square, the Civil Rights movement, and September eleventh. This week we were covering the rise of the Nazi party and World War Two. He told us about this one little country, Denmark, where Hitler had ordered the deportation of all the Jews, but the entire country worked together and evacuated almost the entire Jewish population the night before the arrests were to take place. We watched sections of the movie on it, *Miracle at Midnight*, and then he asked us to put ourselves there and think about what we would have done.

Of course we said we'd have helped. We'd have been part of the resistance because it was the right thing to do.

"But what if you weren't in Denmark? What if you were in Austria, or Poland, or other places where you didn't know if anyone else was helping and there was no power in numbers? What if one person or one family came to you, asking for help, and you knew that if you were caught, you would be sent to a concentration camp?"

It felt unrealistic and one kid said so. "But it happened to many people," Mr. Seecord said. "Corrie Ten Boom's family hid Jews. They were caught and all of them were sent to concentration camps. Most of them died."

Why couldn't we just talk about Greco-Roman pillars and the architecture of ancient ruins?

"Sometimes, the right choice isn't the safe choice." Mr. Seecord looked at me and I thought of Keith, how if he'd made it to school with his guns, I would have have hid and tried to save myself, while Mr. Seecord, with only one arm, would have run straight toward the danger to rescue others.

Was there anything worth dying for? He thought there was. Did I?

When the period finally ended, I headed to lunch with a head full of questions I wanted to ignore. Tasha sat at our table and invited everyone to the barbeque. "It's this Friday night," she said. "Cancel all your plans, because this is important. And the food will be great! We're giving away some cakes, and there will be a—"

She rambled on about all the reasons they should plan to spend Friday evening in a church fellowship hall. "It certainly has more appeal than a blood drive," I said. "I think I'm going to miss it, though."

"What?" She put her hands on her hips. "You can't miss it. You're his best friend!"

I didn't want to tell her I couldn't come because Cameron would be there. I'd succeeded in avoiding him since that day at the clinic. "Chad will have a hundred people wanting to talk to him. I don't need to be there."

"That's not the point!" She crossed her arms. "You need to come to show your support. And whether you talk to him or not, he'll know if you skipped out. What could be more important than being there to show you care and want to help him fight this?"

Did she have to put it that way? Like me showing up was important in the grand scheme of Chad's existence on earth?

"Unless you're going to the hospital to get tested for cancer yourself," she said, pointing a finger at me, "you'd better be there."

"You're kind of pushy for a girl who's not his girlfriend," I said.

She pouted, but then smiled. "Not his girlfriend yet."

"I can't go," I said, and her pouty lip came back out. "There's someone there I can't handle seeing."

"Intriguing." Kendra scooted over closer to Tasha and leaned her elbows on the table to whisper to me, "It's a guy, isn't it? You've got a crush on some guy who will be there."

How had she even heard that from the other side of the table where she'd been sitting? "I'm not telling you who it is," I said, and turned to Tasha. "I can't, okay? I can't be okay in the same room with him for an entire evening."

Her smile was knowing. "Then do whatever you have to do to be okay with it."

"Um...not a clue what that meant."

"Whoever the guy is, you don't have to talk to him," she said. Kendra leaned forward to catch every juicy word, and Tasha smiled at her, then continued. "But if you're feeling insecure about him, it wouldn't hurt for him to see you, from a distance. Especially if you look amazing."

The bell rang and I wadded up my lunch bag. "I don't look amazing. I never look amazing."

Tasha rose and picked up her tray. "Like I said, do what you have to do then."

I stared at her retreating back. What was she talking about? I was just me, and Cameron didn't like me. There wasn't anything I could do to change that, was there?

Mom always liked the phrase about an idea being a "light bulb moment," but I'd never understood it until that second, when a light bulb turned on in my head, out of nowhere. I tossed my trash and rushed into the hallway, searching through the crowd of students at their lockers or on their way to class. Finally, I saw her. Running forward, I caught up just as she neared the gym doors for P.E.

"Alecia," I said, out of breath. "I need your help."

Random Fact: A giraffe's tongue is 20 inches long; it can clean its own ears with it.

Which might be a more appealing activity than shopping for a new outfit when one has zero fashion sense.

CHAPTER THIRTY-SIX

"I can't believe we're doing this," Alecia said, clapping her hands as we entered the mall. "I'm so excited. Aren't you excited?"

I was about as excited as I would be going to the dentist, but I worked up a smile. "Thanks for being willing to help. I have no idea where to start."

"I've always wanted to give you a full makeover." She touched my hair and then looked surprised when I didn't flinch or move away. "Trust me, you're going to look fabulous."

"I'd be happy with normal."

"No, no, no." Alecia did a teen version of skipping, if there was such a thing, and pulled me toward a store with an imbalanced percentage of clothing in a bright shade of orange. "You don't want to look normal. You want to look stunning, attention-grabbing, fabulous. You want every guy at the barbeque Friday night to look at you and not be able to look away."

That sounded terrifying. I pictured Dude and his friends staring and laughing. "Check her out," I could hear him say. "She's trying to look cool. What a dork."

I broke out in a cold sweat even before Alecia had seven tops and four skirts for me to try on. She sent me to the fitting room, which she had to point out to me because I'd never been in the store before. "Go try these on while I pick some more options."

Obeying, that I could do. I put on a skirt that fell to my knees in shimmery waves of purple, and topped it with a sheer black thing that went over a fitted blank fancy kind of tank top. I stepped out and Alecia was already there, more clothes draped over her arm. "That's nice," she said, tapping her finger to her cheek. "But not amazing. And the length doesn't work with your calves. You need longer or shorter. Here, try this." She handed me two of the items from her arms and shooed me back inside.

I took a good look at my calves in the mirror. How on earth did they tell Alecia what kind of skirt I needed? After I tried on the second outfit, a flowy skirt that came to my feet in that bright orange color, with a white top that had sheer sleeves and embroidery all over it, I resisted the urge to organize the pile of clothes in the fitting room by color before going out and being assessed again.

"Oooh, I like that," Alecia said. "We could do a bright orange gloss that would make your eyes pop."

I thought of Chad saying his eyes were bulging out of his head. "I don't think I want my eyes to pop."

She laughed. "What you're wearing might be the one, but try this outfit on, just in case it's even better."

She said that four more times. Like a robot on remote, I put on all the outfits as directed until she decided that the orange and white one was, indeed, the most fabulous for my hair and skin and body type. It felt odd, hearing someone talk so passionately about something other than platelets or bone marrow. We got the outfit and skipped our way to another store to choose the perfect shoes. I told her I had all the shoes I needed.

"This isn't about need," she said loftily. "This is about making an impact."

"You're sure this will be worth it?" I was picturing my savings going down the drain, or rather into the cashier's hands.

Alecia tossed her hair. "Definitely. Wait and see."

She found a pair of heeled shoes that had no backs to them. I shook my head no. I told her I hated high heels and I hated cloppy shoes and refused to wear them. She argued that she "just loved" these and tried to get me to consider them, but when I told her if we bought those I would take them off the moment I got into the fellowship hall and spend the evening barefoot, she caved in and went to another section of the store. We finally compromised on a pair of white sandals with miniature heels and straps around the back to keep them in place.

"Now on to your hair."

"I thought we were done."

"Oh, Vicky, we've barely started!"

I followed, overwhelmed, and finally said, "If this is fun, you must have been dying of boredom all those years we fed the ducks or just hung out."

Her smile was nostalgic. "Oh, it wasn't so bad. Being friends with you was great." She linked her arm through mine and I told myself not to pull away. "It still is."

After getting a sparkly something to pull up part of my hair, and then a pair of earrings that looked kind of lacy, Alecia directed me toward a hair salon. "You know, Vicky, your hair would look so great with a few highlights—"

"No highlights," I said emphatically. I loved my rubber ducks but was not going to walk around with hair that matched them. "Absolutely no highlights."

Alecia sighed and we passed the salon. "Okay, but you've got to let me bring over my straightener and do your hair. And your makeup."

"Don't you have plans for Friday night?"

"Dan and I are coming to the barbeque, of course." She sighed again. "Just because we aren't living at the clinic doesn't mean we aren't all good friends anymore. We'll be there to show our support, you can count on it!"

"Great." People were so confusing sometimes. I didn't think I would ever figure out the human race in general and Alecia in particular. Chad would tell me that's okay, and maybe it was.

When Friday rolled around, Alecia was true to her word. She came over two hours early and though I thought that was far too much time, she used every minute to transform me into what she was sure—and I hoped—looked fabulous.

I rode with her and Dan to the church and then stood outside the fellowship hall, trembling and clinging to my little white purse/bag bought for just this occasion. My toenails and fingernails were painted, my lips were shimmery, my face was covered in at least two layers of paint, and my hair had been gooed and brushed and straightened until it hung glossy and perfect down over my shoulders, except for one little braid pulled back on the left side and secured with the sparkly flower.

This was meant to be my moment. Most girls wait for the prom, but I was supposed to have mine at a barbeque. I hoped Cameron would see me before I sat down with a plate and likely spilled barbeque sauce all down the front of my perfect white shirt. Then again, I hoped he wouldn't see me. I hoped he wasn't there at all. But then that would have wasted all this effort.

"Are you coming?" Alecia peeked her head back outside. "I thought you were right behind us." She looked me over. "Oh my goodness, you're scared, aren't you?"

Petrified. Nervous to the point of being sick. I couldn't even tug on my hair, too afraid of messing up Alecia's work. I just nodded and she came to stand in front of me, a motherly smile on her face. "Really, Vicky, you look great. I promise. Everyone's going to think so."

I didn't want everyone thinking about me, looking at me. "Can I go home?"

"No." She pulled me toward the door. "I am your fairy godmother and I say you cannot waste my magic one more minute. Get in there and make an appearance!"

By then she had me just inside the door. Dan called her over to the drink table and she disappeared before I could beg her not to leave my side. I wasn't in kindergarten anymore, but I gladly would have hidden behind her just then. I looked for someone tall or large who I could stand behind until I got the nerve to cross the room, and that's when I saw him.

Before I could move, before I could look away so he didn't catch me staring, Cameron turned and glanced past me and then his eyes came right back and locked with mine. His mouth dropped open a little, and then he was coming my way.

Random Fact: More people die of heart attacks on Mondays than any other day of the week.

It figures that I was going to die of a heart attack on a Friday, when everybody else was having fun.

CHAPTER THIRTY-SEVEN

In the movies, when the girl has her big moment, there's music playing, and she's surrounded by the hazy glow of excitement in the air. Her heart is pounding and she's terrified but it's okay because the guy is going to say just the right thing, his eyes are going to shine, and everything will work out as it should, happily ever after and all that.

My moment seriously missed the mark. Music was playing, some Christian song about overcoming. The only haze in the air came from the grill near the kitchen area of the fellowship hall. I was indeed terrified and my heart was pounding, but it wasn't okay because Cameron Carlson strode toward me with a glare in his eye instead of a gleam, and his scowl promised everything but happily ever after.

"Hi, Cameron," I said feebly when he got within two feet of me. He didn't keep his distance but stepped closer, until we were only inches apart. His gaze took in my face, then my hair, then dropped all the way to my fancy new shoes and back up to my eyelashes made extra long and thick by Alecia's super-mega blah blah blah mascara.

"Victoria." He said it like I was a stranger. I guess that was the idea of the whole makeover thing, to be someone new, but new wasn't getting the desired positive response.

"What happened to you?" he asked, like I'd walked in with a black eye.

Chad walked toward us from the side. "Hey, Vicks, you look fantastic!" I hadn't seen him out of a chair in so long, he seemed tall. He wore a ball cap with jeans and a t-shirt, and aside from being leaner than before, he looked like any other teen guy. Normal. Funny how deceptive that word can be.

"Vicky, wow." Tasha was at his side, her own hair in tight curls, a shiny gloss looking like it belonged on her lips. She beamed at me, but I think it was just leftover light from her being with Chad. "What a great outfit. And I love your hair!"

"Thanks." I caught myself tugging at it and put my hands at my sides. We stood for an awkward moment or two while Chad and Tasha looked from my insecure fidgeting to Cameron's stony silence. Alecia bounced up and put an arm around me. Cameron stared her down like she'd attacked me, but she didn't seem to notice.

"Doesn't she look fabulous?" Alecia gushed. "I will accept all compliments for my fairy godmother work. Our dear friend Vicky is destined to impress the guy of her dreams tonight!"

I closed my eyes and imagined myself in my bathtub.

"That's what this is for?" Cameron asked. I opened my eyes to see him glaring at Chad. "Are you the reason for this?"

"Me?" Chad put his hands out in a don't-know-what-you're-talking-about gesture. The music felt too loud and the smell of barbeque was overwhelming. "The reason for what?"

"She doesn't look like herself." He motioned toward me, but since he was standing so close, his hand brushed against my midriff. Normal people would just take a step back, but I froze like a corpse. He turned red but looked me in the eye. "You've always been yourself. Why are you trying to be someone else?"

"She's not." Alecia brushed my hair off my shoulder like she owned it. "She's a fabulous version of herself. She looks great."

"She's always looked great," Cameron said. Everyone's eyebrows went up: mine, Alecia's, even Chad's and Tasha's. "She's never needed any of that extra stuff, and she doesn't need it now." He pointed at Chad. "Not for you. Not for anybody."

He stormed off to the line of tables loaded with pulled pork, buns, and huge bottles of mayonnaise and ketchup. We watched him pile a plate with a sandwich, then move on to the table with chips and dip, then to the cookies. He got a bottled water and went and sat on a large windowsill ledge. Alone. When he looked our way and saw us all staring, he stood and walked out of the room, leaving his plate and water on the ledge.

"What's eating him?" Tasha asked. She turned to Chad. "Is he mad at you about something?"

"I have no idea." Chad shrugged. "But I'm not going to let it ruin my night. In fact, I'm going to go sit in his spot by the window and eat his sandwich."

She laughed and they walked off together, her arm threaded through his.

"I sure hope you weren't doing all this to impress Cameron," Alecia said. I hadn't unfrozen from the touch yet so couldn't get any stiffer. She laughed at her own comment. "Because he sure seems to like the old Vicky best. I guess if you want to get to him, you'd better get your sweatpants out and mess up your hair."

Dan waved at her from across the room and she gave me one more side hug. "I'm off to make my own impression. I hope whoever you came here for is just waiting for me to run off so he can come tell you how gorgeous you are."

She bounced away toward Dan and I stood there, still not ten feet into the room, acceptable now to everybody in sight but feeling more out of place than I ever had in my life.

With a little sob, I pivoted on my perfect new shoes and did what I'm good at. I ran away.

Random Fact: The human brain is one of the most complex things known to man, according to the human brain.

And it's nothing compared to the complexity of the human heart.

CHAPTER THIRTY-EIGHT

I was at the door when it opened and Shane and Kendra appeared. "You came," I said, stating the obvious fact that they were there rather than the equally obvious fact that I'd nearly run them over.

Kendra looked around nervously. "Tasha bribed us with the promise of a whole table of cookies."

"Come on in." The last thing I wanted to do was stay and play hostess, but I couldn't just leave them. I knew too well how it felt to be a stranger in a crowd where everyone seemed to know each other. I led them, slowly so Shane could keep up, across the room and introduced them to kids from the youth group I'd met at the hospital. Chad and Tasha invited them to sit at their table once they got food, so I got them settled and then made some excuse about needing to get some air. At that point I was closer to the rear door than the front, so I slipped out the back.

The spring air was cool but not cold. I took a few steps to the side away from the door and leaned my back against the wall. The harsh concrete probably snagged my pretty new shirt but what difference did it make? I took in several deep breaths, my eyes closed, my heart hurting. I thought being a kid had been hard, but in the end, I could always find a quiet place and put my toys in perfect, orderly rows. Now the things I wanted in order had to do with other people, and they weren't aligning themselves in an orderly way at all. If they were ducks, they'd be bonking into each other and then floating off in all sorts of directions.

What was I to do? I didn't want to be a hermit for the rest of my life, but why did people have to be so complicated?

"I'm sorry."

I jumped at least two feet from the wall and left one of my shoes behind. Cameron picked it up and held it out to me. For a second, it looked like he might drop to one knee like Prince Charming and slip it on my foot, but I reached out and snatched it and put it back on myself. I didn't need any chivalry. Not from him.

"I shouldn't have let into you like that," he said, his eyes down like he found my feet interesting. "You do look very pretty. I just—seeing you so different, it just—knowing why—"

I crossed my arms, not bothering to hide my frustration. It was better than bursting into tears or some other humiliating expression of emotion. "Am I supposed to understand anything you're saying?"

"If I was a good brother, I'd be happy for him. Happy he had someone wonderful to help him through this time. I'd want him to have that, even if it meant—"

For some reason, I thought about his plate of food that Chad ate. "You didn't eat your food," I said. "Aren't you hungry?"

"No. Did you eat?"

"No." *Who could eat at a time like this?* My one shoe felt crooked. I adjusted my foot.

"Aren't you hungry?" he asked.

"No, and even if I was, I wouldn't want to spill something on my new top. It's white." As if he couldn't tell that. I was the queen of boring conversation.

"See? That's just it."

"Just what?"

He put his hand toward me as if pointing out an exhibit. "You aren't the type to avoid eating just to protect your clothes. You don't pretend to be something you're not to prove yourself. You've always been true to who you are. It's one of the things I've always admired about you, and I hate to see it change. It's so...appealing."

"That's a stupid thing to say." I turned my back on him. "You don't even want to be my friend. You can't stand to be anywhere near me."

His voice came from close behind me. "I never said that."

"Oh, yes you did." I was near tears now. "And if my real self is so abhorrent to you..." I stopped. Abhorrent was one of those words I'd read but wasn't sure how to pronounce. I needed to stick with words I knew how to say. It would be worse than humiliating to be laughed at as you're baring your soul because you can't speak correctly. "Then why mind me being something different?"

"What difference does it make if I mind or not?" His voice faded somewhat, as if he'd stepped away from me back to the wall. "All that matters is what Chad thinks."

I wished I knew how to snort like Tasha. I whirled to face him. "Would you get off the Chad thing? He and Tasha are together, okay? She's all mushy around him and I'm pretty sure he likes her, so—"

Cameron came and stood right in front of me. "But in the clinic he said—"

"He was joking about me telling him Tasha thought I was his girlfriend." I put my hands on my hips and could feel my bottom lip puckering out in a pout. Good grief, did dressing like Alecia make me naturally do her facial expressions as well? "If you're going to eavesdrop, you should listen longer."

His eyes searched mine. "But Alecia said...so are you telling me you're not Chad's girlfriend, but you'd like to be?"

"Are you dense?"

"Maybe." His gaze traveled over my face and my heart started pumping too fast to be normal. "Alecia said you did this whole new look hoping to impress a guy. I assumed it was Chad."

"Obviously from your big scene inside," I said. How could I be so mad at him and still have this weird desire to throw my arms around him? That was not sensible. What was happening to me? "You should apologize to him."

"I will." He stared at me.

I couldn't take it. "Now."

He looked back at the door, then at me again. "Now?"

I nodded. I could handle his frustration better than whatever was in his eyes right then. He'd never looked at me like that before, and I didn't know what to think or what to do. I wanted to run away.

"Will you promise to stay right here till I get back?"

"I want to go home."

"Just stay till I get back." He put his hand out and almost touched my arm. "Promise?"

I sucked in a deep breath. "Okay."

He went inside and I waited, alternating my weight first on one sore foot, then the other. I was taking these shoes back to the store tomorrow. When he reappeared and came toward me, I blurted out the first thing I could think of. "You should be ashamed of yourself, fussing at your brother his one night out having fun."

"You're right. I am." He smiled at me. It was most unnerving.

"Well, I think—"

"Who's the guy?"

I looked at the door behind him, then at his hair, then down at his shoes. They weren't new or fancy. "What guy?"

"The guy you were hoping to impress tonight."

Had Alecia said something to him? He kept smiling at me. I wished he'd stop. "It doesn't matter. It didn't work."

Cameron took a step closer. I took a step back. "Whoever he is, if he doesn't want to spend all evening looking at you, he's an idiot."

I sniffed. "That's not funny."

"It wasn't meant to be." He reached up and touched the little braid in my hair.

I pushed his hand away. "Why don't you go back inside? You said being my friend was too hard. So go be around someone it's not hard to be friends with."

I turned but he caught me by the shoulders from behind. When he spoke, his breath moved my hair like a breeze and brushed against my neck. "Don't you get it, Victoria? Being your friend is too hard because I don't want to be just your friend. I've tried to avoid you for months because I thought you and Chad..."

I felt light-headed. What was he saying?

"I know it's not the right time." His fingers on my shoulders made tiny shivery fish swim all up and down my arms. "Chad's got his big three weeks of final treatment coming up, and I know he'll need you to be there for him." He chuckled and the shivers ran across and down my back. "I'm not such a selfish guy that I'd try to steal a cancer patient's best friend. But when it's over, Victoria, you and I are going to have a talk."

His hands released me. I wanted to turn and look at his eyes, to see for myself if he was joking or not. But I could not move. My feet felt cemented to the pavement.

His footsteps receded toward the door, but then came close again. "And Victoria," he said near my ear. I bit my cheek, tugged my hair, and rocked from one foot to the other all at the same time. "In the hopes that maybe it was me, there's no way you could look any prettier than you do when you're just being you."

I heard him walk away. The door creaked open then closed. My lungs heaved for air and I put a hand to my heart. Had he really meant it? Had he meant what I thought he meant?

Three weeks. I'd have to wait three weeks to find out.

Random Fact: For one day, a section of a hospital in Ottawa, Canada became international territory so a Dutch Princess could be born a full Dutch citizen (a requirement to be a Dutch Princess). Every year the Netherlands sends Canada a gift of tulips to show their gratitude.

There's hope for humanity yet.

CHAPTER THIRTY-NINE

Chad was far from excited about spending another three weeks checked into the hospital, so we tried to make it as non-miserable as possible for him. We rotated our visits so he would rarely be alone. His parents brought movies and snacks. Cameron played games on his tablet with him. Tasha brought her Bible and they studied together. I just sat with him, but that was needed too. With me, he talked about his fears and how hard it was, things he kept hidden from the others.

We all gave our lives to Chad those three weeks in April, while he fought for his own life. The chance to have a future. A future and a hope, as Tasha put it. Chad read the entire Bible those three weeks, as he said he would. He worked on his essay, and said he had his outline and some notes, but the chemo symptoms kept him from finishing it. He gave it to Tasha and she cried reading it. She offered it to me, but I declined. My own essay did not have a word, did not have even a blank sheet of paper designated for ideas yet. I could listen to Chad talk about life and death for his sake, but still refused to think about it on my own.

The days passed in a blur of nausea and headaches and the celebration of tiny accomplishments like Chad walking fifteen feet down the hallway and back, or keeping his dinner down. People came and prayed and brought gifts and more casseroles. Chad's wall filled up with cards and pictures the church kids drew for him. I wondered if he was aware enough to know how loved he was. How many people cared about his life.

Then one day, it was over. The doctor came into Chad's room that third Saturday. We were all there, celebrating his first day after the final chemo. The doctor smiled, a real smile, and said, "Chad, I'm happy to tell you that you are cancer free."

The room was silent and time seemed to stop. Even after so many weeks of fighting and so many hopes, it seemed impossible to be hearing those words. The doctor finally laughed out loud, and Chad gave a big whoop of victory, and we all cheered and cried and hugged and cried some more. I didn't care that people were touching me or that the room was reverberating with noise or that chaos reigned. Chad was going to live. He was going to be okay.

He got released from the hospital a few hours after that. I helped him pack up his cards and pictures and gifts. Tasha was at his house by then helping Mrs. Carlson bake a big welcome home cake. Cameron was at home, too, and I felt a burning right between my ribs at the thought of what he might say after I got there that night.

I kept packing to keep my nervousness at bay. When I got to the windowsill, to our ducks, I asked Chad if he wanted me to take them back home with me.

"No way," he said. "They're going on my windowsill in my room." He stood and wobbled a little. I went over to help steady him, my arm around his waist and a hand against his chest. He smiled down at me. "Never thought I'd see the day when you would touch someone on purpose. You've really changed, Vicks, in a lot of good ways."

"So have you." I smiled back. "I really like Tasha, by the way."

He roughed up my hair. His own was just peach fuzz and I had the urge to touch it and see what it felt like. "Just so you know," he said. "No matter what happens with Tasha, I don't want to lose my best friend, okay?"

I nodded, smiling on the inside. Maybe some things never would change.

"Do you remember the counselor who came to visit back in between my ICU adventures?" he asked.

A nurse came in pushing a wheelchair. "Standard procedure," she said before Chad could object.

"I wouldn't call them adventures," I commented as Chad worked his way over to the chair and dropped into it. "But yes, I remember her."

"Mom told me the other day that the counselor said if I got to the point where I was going to die—"

I cringed and covered by grabbing his bag of stuff and heading out the door first.

The nurse followed, pushing Chad. "If I was going to die," he repeated, "it would be good for the people who love me to come and give me permission."

How long would it be before he'd realize he was going to live and stop talking about this? "Give you permission?"

"Yeah, because sometimes people hold on too long because they feel bad about leaving others behind. So she said to say something like, 'It's okay. You can go now.'"

"And you're telling me this sad story because...?"

The entrance doors to the hospital slid open and fresh air circled around us like a hug. Chad breathed in deep and sighed. "I don't know. I guess I was just thinking this morning how nice it was that nobody had to say that to me. That I got to stay."

My eyes stung. I told myself it was pollen in the air. I reached over and rubbed the fuzz on his head. "I'm glad you got to stay, too. Now stop being depressing and let's go have a party."

He laughed. "You're on. To the car, Nurse, double quick!"

I drove him home. It took awhile for him to walk from the car to his front door. "I'm such a wuss," he said, a little out of breath.

"You're just weak from the chemo. It'll pass in a couple of days and you'll feel great."

He stopped at the door and looked down at me. "I will, won't I?" His eyes held wonder. "This isn't just a break before I go back for more. I'm done."

"You're done. You won."

"I won," he whispered. He threw the door open and shouted, "I won!"

A chorus of cheers responded from the inside and he jerked back. I laughed. The house was full to overflowing with school friends and church friends and extended family and quite a few strangers, perhaps people who wandered in because they could feel the joy all the way out to the street.

We celebrated that night. My own parents were there, and Alex, who ate three pieces of cake and made himself sick. Alecia and Dan stayed late into the night and got in on the fun of Chad telling jokes to see if he could get Tasha to snort. Shane and Kendra and a few other people from the freak table came to meet Chad and see if he was odd enough to be invited to join us. There really wasn't much about Chad that was abnormal, but his current peach fuzz head looked unusual enough that they all felt comfortable around him.

I wanted to sing for happiness, but as I'm a terrible singer, I spared everyone the trauma of listening to me and just hummed on the inside as I made my way to Chad's room with his bag. I set his cards up in a perfect line across the top of his desk and stacked the pictures for him to look at later. At the bottom of the bag I found our ducks, and set them carefully on his windowsill, arranging each until it stood exactly where it should.

"Hey, Victoria." Cameron came into the room and the noise downstairs faded behind the ringing in my ears.

I bit my lip. "Hey, Cameron."

"We made it," he said, coming to stand beside me. He nudged Chad's duck slightly off kilter. I moved it back and he smiled. "We got through and there's no more cancer. I'm finding it kind of hard to believe."

"Me too. But it's great."

"Very great."

I waited for him to say something important, but even still, when he did, it took me by surprise. "Do you think it would be okay for a guy to ask out his little brother's best friend?"

My heart thundered. "It couldn't hurt to ask," I said. "What's the worst that could happen?"

He grinned and moved Chad's duck half an inch to the side. "She could laugh in his face and reject him."

I moved it back and flicked his hand when he tried a third time. "She wouldn't do that if she was a nice person at all. She'd care about his feelings."

His hand blocked mine and he moved my duck. "Then she might say no."

I tried to put it back but he captured both my hands. "I guess that's a risk you'd have to be willing to take," I said.

"Would you, Victoria?" He tugged on my hands until I looked him in the face. "Would you go out with me sometime? I can't this weekend because of work, but next weekend maybe?"

"Just a second." I pulled my hands free and put my duck back in place. He laughed and probably thought I was being obsessive, but in truth I was giving myself something to do while I tried to get my feelings under control. Cameron Carlson had just asked me out. That was huge, like a bubble expanding inside me. I was afraid it would burst and my emotions would spurt out everywhere. Settling the duck did nothing to settle my heart, but when I looked at him, my shy smile grew until it matched his. "Yes."

"Yes? Really?"

"I'd like to go out with you."

He took one of my hands back in his again. "I'm really glad to hear that. Let's go down and celebrate with some cake."

We got down the stairs and he didn't release my hand. I wanted him to, but didn't want him to, and finally decided to stop deciding and just enjoy it. I was going on a date with Cameron Carlson, next weekend!

Or so I thought.

Random Fact: Anatidaephobia is the fear that somewhere, somehow, a duck is watching you.

That's not a fear; that's a comfort.

CHAPTER FORTY

Monday was Chad's first day back at school. It was a special day, and I wanted to make it a big deal. He started out wearing his ball cap, but I convinced him to take if off and let his buzz look show. I was proud of the short hairs sticking out all over his head. They meant he had made it and was healing. They meant he'd won, and I wanted everyone to see it.

"Check it out." I pointed to the wall above the entrance doors as we neared the school building. "I bet the cheerleaders made it for you."

A banner hung over the doors. "Welcome back, Chad!" he read. "Nice bubble letters. So I guess having cancer promises instant popularity."

"Not exactly instant." I parked and before we could get out of the car, students were at Chad's door. "But impressive."

The crowd escorted Chad inside and he got pats on the back and lots of hugs as he made his way down the hallway to his locker. He opened it and the mob around him backed away.

I laughed and held my nose. "Ten week old banana. Appealing."

Tasha merged through the traffic toward us. "Chad, you're here!" She put her arms out to hug him, then drew back. "What is that awful smell?"

Chad grabbed a brown lunch bag in his locker and used it to mop up the rotting banana. "I like to keep my lunch leftovers in my locker, in case I get hungry later."

"What's in the bag?"

He held the bag, now covered in banana goop, out at arms length and everyone made a wide path from him to a trash can. "I don't even want to know."

We walked with him to homeroom, where he got a standing ovation, which was cool. I didn't know what happened in his other classes, but in history, they cheered as he came in the room. I loved it.

"I wish they'd stop acting like I did something amazing," Chad commented, sliding into a desk beside me.

"But you did do something amazing."

"I just survived, that's all."

"It was much more than that." I put my backpack on the ground. "But even if it wasn't, surviving is something to celebrate, isn't it? If I'd gone through ten weeks of treatments and you heard I was cancer free, wouldn't you think it was important?"

He looked at me while Mr. Seecord called the class to order. "Yeah, I guess I would," he said.

I smiled and whispered, "Then live it up."

At lunch, I took Chad to the freak table to introduce him to any of the ones he hadn't met yet. They invited him to stay, but I said no. "I want him to myself for awhile," I said. "I'll share him soon."

I led the way to an empty table but Chad touched my arm and inclined his head toward the exit door. I followed him outside, curious. "Where are we going?"

"I got special permission for us to eat outside this week." He headed for a bench across the grassy field surrounding the school building.

"No way."

"Way. I told the principal I really missed the sunshine while I was in the hospital, and the weather was so nice, etcetera, etcetera, and here we are." He winked at me and I laughed. "And though it's true that the weather is great, and I truly did miss sunshine, I have ulterior motives for us being out here."

I sat beside him on the bench and unpacked my lunch. "If I didn't know better, I'd think you were flirting with me."

"I'll leave that to Cameron." I blushed and he grinned. "We, my friend, are on a hunt for clues."

Stupid wheat sandwich. When I was an adult, I was eating only the white stuff, forever. "Clues about what?"

"I want to find Keith's bomb."

"Seriously?" I took a bite. Tuna. I really should ask Mom if I could start packing my own lunch. "You think it really exists?"

"I don't know." He gave a casual shrug. "But it's more interesting to think about than the periodic table, or the hundred other things I need to catch up on."

"True. Where do you think it could be?" I waved my hand across the field. "Mr. Seecord said he's been over the whole field with a metal detector."

"What if he didn't use metal?"

"Can you make a bomb without metal?"

Chad chomped on a carrot stick. His lunch looked overboard on the healthy side. His Mom must have vetoed his usual choices. "I am not a bomb-making expert," he said, "so instead of guessing what it was made of, let's brainstorm about where he could have hidden it. If you had a bomb, where would you put it—a place that wouldn't be found for a year?"

"I'd hide it in the gym."

Chad eyed the building. "I'd put it in my locker."

"They emptied Keith's locker." I washed down the tuna with my bottled water.

"They searched the gym top to bottom."

"Good point."

He leaned forward. "Maybe it's underneath this bench," he said ominously, and though I laughed, I still had the urge to bend over and check.

Lunch passed too quickly, without any legitimate ideas for finding Keith's possibly nonexistent bomb, though Chad promised we would visit the subject again. And we did. Every day that week, we ate our lunch outside—me getting to enjoy the perks of being best friends with the guy Alecia called the school's newest golden boy (which made no sense to me since his skin was pasty white from all those weeks in the hospital). During lunch we discussed our theories on where it might be. After school, we'd hunt for the few minutes it took for the student body to clear out, before us hanging around caused suspicion. We scoured the area underneath the gym bleachers until Coach Appleton found us and made a big speech about students making out down there. We snooped around the principal's office and the teacher's lounge. We tapped the wall that had been remodeled to hold the school intercom system, and poked around all the fire extinguishers.

"This is totally useless, you know," I said on Thursday afternoon. "We're never going to find anything."

"Don't say that." Chad's head was hidden behind the school trophy case and his voice came through garbled. "We've found two hats, one glove, lots of used gum, and now..." He emerged with a rubber chicken in hand and I burst out laughing. "Someone probably misses this thing."

"I give up," I said. "Let's go home."

"Want to keep the chicken?"

"It's got somebody's old band-aid stuck to it. That's disgusting."

"Okay." He tossed it back behind the trophy case. "I need to go anyway. Got to prepare for tomorrow."

"What's happening tomorrow?"

He smiled and wiggled his fingers at me. "You'll have to wait and find out."

Random Fact: Oreos are actually a knock-off of a cookie brand called Hydrox that was created 4 years before the Oreo. People assumed Hydrox was the knock-off as Oreos became immensely popular.

Popularity is a strange, unpredictable beast.

CHAPTER FORTY-ONE

The next day I found out why Chad hadn't told me what he was doing. I would have skipped school.

Mr. Seecord did our usual history class routine, but about ten minutes before the bell, he told us to put our books away and clear our desks. Kids around me moaned about a pop quiz, but when Mr. Seecord summoned Chad up front, I was sure I knew what was coming. I raised my hand. "Can I go use the restroom?"

Chad turned and leveled me with a look. "You stay right there, Victoria Dane."

When the class quieted down, after taking an inordinate amount of time to produce a minimal amount of order out of their books and such, Mr. Seecord put his one hand on Chad's shoulder and said, "I know your essay isn't due until next month, but Chad has finished his, and I want him to read it to you. Maybe you'll find some inspiration."

We had spent a whole week not talking about death. I had loved every sunny, funny minute of it. Why did he have to ruin it now?

Chad held a sheet of typing paper in front of him and cleared his throat. "Some people don't like to talk about dying." He glanced at me. I glared back. "But it's a part of life. It may not be a part we look forward to, but it's there. We don't know when we will die, or how, but death is waiting for each of us."

Dad would say you could hear a pin drop, but no one dropped a pin. Chad looked up from his paper. "I know I sound morbid, but stick with me."

He focused back on his paper and continued. "In the hospital, with cancer eating away at my body, I had a lot of time to think about Mr. Seecord's question on what was worth dying for. When you're closed inside an MRI machine, or having needles probe your spinal fluid, or ingesting poison on purpose, you don't tend to think about sports or who is popular or the next party. You think about death. And life. And you wonder what's the point."

I closed my eyes and tried to shut everything out, but Chad's words pushed through. I couldn't get away.

"That's what it comes down to, doesn't it?" he said. "To find out what's worth dying for or living for, you have to find out what the point of all of this is. Why are we here? Is life just some big accident? If it is, I can't find any purpose in it. But what if it's not? What if we were made for a reason, and our lives matter? What if there is purpose in every person's existence, and our choices are significant? If that is true, a life well lived isn't wasted, whether a person gets ten years or a hundred."

No one moved. Normally, Jordan Phelps would be snickering by now, and Rodney Johnson would be flicking a pencil or throwing a paper airplane while Mr. Seecord wasn't looking. But Chad wasn't normal anymore. Whatever he had to say about death was valid, because he'd been so close to it and come back.

"A hope, a purpose that is worth dying for, is also worth living for. I found that hope in Jesus, and I'm going to follow Him with whatever life I have left." He looked around the room. "I say whatever life I have left because the truth is that the cancer could come back. I've had it once, and I'll carry that with me forever. Already, if my head starts to hurt or I wake up sore, it's the first thing I think of. But I refuse to live scared. And I refuse to live with no purpose. Life, the chance to really live it, is a gift. With God's help, I'm going to live a life that means something. I'm going to make choices that matter." He smiled over at Mr. Seecord. "Even if the right choice isn't always the safe one."

Mr. Seecord smiled back. I wiped my eyes. No wonder Tasha had cried when she read this. Somewhere between pre-cancer and post-cancer, Chad Carlson had become a man.

"Most of us won't have the option of knowing when we'll die or how. The goal shouldn't be to avoid it, because that's impossible. Our goal shouldn't even be to delay it as much as we can if it means our lives become fearful and obsessed with tofu or yoga or stuff that gives empty promises." He shrugged and grinned my way. "A friend of mine who collects random facts once told me that James Fixx, the man who popularized jogging in America, died of a heart attack while running. Go figure."

A few students chuckled along with Chad. He looked at his paper, but I wondered if he had stopped reading and was just talking at that point. "Trying to avoid death isn't something worth living for. Living is worth living for. And I'm going to live every day that I have left. I have been given a future and a hope, and I don't want to waste it."

He looked over his paper, then flipped it to the back, which was blank. He shrugged. "That's it, I guess."

The bell rang but no one budged. Mr. Seecord dismissed the class but it was as if all the students felt the same way I did. I didn't know what to do. How to respond. The seconds dragged on and finally I stood to my feet and gathered my books, but instead of walking to the door, I made my way down the row toward Chad. I set my books on the front desk in the row, then reached out and gave my best friend a hug.

Chad went stiff, which made me smile. "Victoria Dane," he said. "I think that was a first."

"You're right."

He messed up my hair. "I am truly honored."

I noticed a line had formed behind me, so I collected my books and headed for the door, turning at it to see the other students following my example. The girls hugged him. The guys smacked him on the shoulder or gave him a high five, or shook his hand. I felt I was witnessing something sacred.

It was a beautiful moment in a week I would never forget.

Random Fact: Every human spent about half an hour as a single cell.

And then we become over a trillion cells. Life is amazing.

CHAPTER FORTY-TWO

"It's too beautiful to go back inside." I dropped my apple core into my lunch bag and flopped off the bench and onto the grass. "Just one more minute."

"We're going to be late," Chad warned, but I knew he didn't want to go any more than I did. This sunny day with a breeze was a treasure, our final one, because after today, the principal said we'd have to start eating in the cafeteria again like normal students. "I wish we had history next instead of phys ed. Coach Appleton isn't going to be as understanding as Mr. Seecord would be."

I glanced from the grass at my feet across the field and sidewalks to the western side of the school building. Three classrooms had windows facing us. The first was Mr. Rupert's algebra class, which I found baffling to the extreme. Typically I enjoyed math, since it was all about putting numbers in order, but algebra turned math into a foreign language. The farthest window was for woodwork or some other elective I had no intention of taking, and the middle window was Mr. Seecord's classroom. Even with the glare the sun cast off the window, we could see him beginning class inside.

With a sigh, I packed up the rest of my trash and dusted the grass off my jeans. "Alecia would be horrified to see my pants touching the natural elements. At least I didn't get my white shirt dirty." I was wearing the embroidered top from the barbeque. "I've worn this shirt three times now and haven't spilled anything on it yet. The stress of waiting for the inevitable is killing me."

Chad took my bag of trash and stuffed it inside his. He grinned at me and mimicked Alecia's voice. "But if you care a little, Victoria, you could be pretty. Not just pretty—you could be fabulous."

I laughed and grabbed the bag out of his hand. "Why does that make me want to smear ketchup all over this shirt?"

His smile changed. "You're fine just as you are."

I didn't know what to say to that. I blushed and stammered, "So do you think we'll get a detention?"

Chad didn't answer. When I looked his way, his smile had dropped and his brows were tight. Did he have a headache? I had the hospital number programmed into my phone in case he had a relapse. "Chad? What's the matter?"

His gaze was past me, toward the school building. I turned and followed his line of sight to the parking lot in front of the school. My mouth dropped open but no sound came out.

Chad's voice had no tone. "It's him," he said.

I started shaking on the inside. "No, it can't be. He's locked up."

"I know his walk, Vicks. It's Keith."

I squinted. Faded dark jeans and a black t-shirt. Oily dark hair down to his hunched shoulders. A skull tattoo on the bicep of his right arm. It couldn't be anyone but him. "He's headed for the school entrance."

Chad looked at me. "You know what that means."

"No. Maybe it doesn't. Maybe he wants to apologize. Or say goodbye. His mom said when he got out, they were moving, and my mom said—"

Chad stood. "Vicks, look. He's got a duffle bag."

I jumped up next to him and watched in horror as Keith stopped in a handicapped parking space just before the sidewalk to the school entrance. He dropped his bag to the ground and unzipped it. When he pulled out a long gun, I grabbed Chad's arm and held tight to keep from running away.

Chad dropped the lunch bag we'd been fighting over. It crumpled at our feet but neither of us moved to pick it up. "We have to call the police."

Even my voice shook. "They won't get here in time."

Keith strapped the gun over his right shoulder. He got a knife from the bag and tucked it into his pants. Then he pulled a phone from his pocket and his fingers tapped the screen, like he was sending a text.

"Do you think he's telling someone else to come? Maybe whoever sent the letter?"

"I don't know," Chad said, "but I'm not waiting until he starts shooting." His mouth was a grim line. "We have to stop him. Now."

Fact: A hero is a person who, in the face of danger and adversity or from a position of weakness, displays courage or self-sacrifice for some greater good. Historically, the first heroes displayed courage or excellence as warriors. The word's meaning was later extended to include moral excellence.

I am not a hero.

CHAPTER FORTY-THREE

"Wait. No." I grabbed his arm. "Chad, no. We can—"

He turned and took me by the upper arms and looked into my eyes. "Sometimes the right choice isn't the safe one." He released me, turned on his heel, and started running.

I took off after him but he stopped, turned, and grabbed my arms again. "Call nine-one-one and tell them everything you see," Chad said. His voice was forceful. "You have to stay here. You can't tell them what they need to know if you're with me and close enough for Keith to see you. I need you to do this, okay?"

I hesitated.

"Do this for me, Vicks. Please." Then he did something that terrified me. He put his hands on the sides of my face and looked at me for one long moment, his eyes wet, before he leaned in and kissed me on the forehead. I didn't have time to process or panic over what it meant before he tore off across the field toward the school, far enough to the right that Keith wouldn't see him.

I was screaming on the inside. My hands shook so much, it took me three tries to dial the number.

"Nine-one-one, what is your emergency?"

"He's back!" I whispered with urgency into the phone. "He's got a gun and a knife, and he just got another gun out of his bag! He's walking across the sidewalk toward the school entrance doors. You have to send the police out here right now! He's going to kill people. You have to stop him!"

"Calm down," the voice said and I wanted to shout at her. "What is your name?"

"My name isn't important!" I was running now, straight for Mr. Seecord's window. "It's Keith's name that matters. He's back at our school!"

"Keith Childers?" The voice on the phone was no longer deadpan. Everyone in town, especially the emergency responders, remembered what happened last year. "He got put in juvenile detention."

"Well, he's here now! Hurry!" I had almost reached the wall of the building. I threw the phone to the grass and pounded on the window, shrieking. For once, I wanted everyone to look at me. I needed them all to hear.

Mr. Seecord was inside, phone in hand. His worried gaze rose to me and he quickly rushed across the room. He opened the window from the inside. "Victoria, what—"

I didn't let him ask his question. "Keith is coming into the school through the front entrance." I took in heaving gulps of air. Kids in the room stood in panic. Mr. Seecord yelled for them to get back in their desks and be silent. They obeyed, all their wide, terrified eyes trained on me. "Chad is going to try to stop him. He'll get killed!" All around the room, cell phones emerged. Students started calling and texting and I heard the same fear in their voices as came out of mine. "Please do something!"

Mr. Seecord showed me his phone. He'd received a text. "I'm here and it's still here."

"That's from him," I said. My throat tightened up. "He means the bomb, doesn't he?"

"We need to get to the school intercom." He ordered his students to line up against the wall behind him, then turned back to me. "There's one in the gym that works throughout the school. Do you think you could get there?" He handed me a key on a photo keychain and leaned forward so only I could hear. "You and I are the only ones who know about the bomb threat. We have to get the students out of the building. Tell them to climb out the windows and run in a zigzag pattern toward the trees across the field. Tell them if they hear shooting to drop to the ground."

I stopped thinking of how dangerous it would be, how Mr. Seecord shouldn't be asking me to risk my life. "The right choice," I said.

He nodded.

"You'll lead the students to safety?" I asked.

"No." His eyes glinted dark. "I'm going to stop that boy from killing my kids." He gripped my hand. "Go," he said.

I thought of arguing that he didn't have a weapon. He didn't even have two arms. Instead, while he quickly gave orders to the students in his class to file out the window one at a time and run, I picked up my own feet and ran for my life.

No, not for my life. For Chad's life. For Mr. Seecord's. For us all.

Random Fact: A dime has 118 ridges around the edge.

Some days random facts are very, very unimportant.

CHAPTER FORTY-FOUR

Mr. Seecord's students ran from the building toward the trees, most of them crying into their cell phones to frantic parents or friends or emergency operators. I stayed close to the brick walls of the school building and tried to make a plan. The gym had two doors connecting it to the main hallway. One was in the front, near the entrance. The other was in the back, across from the last classroom. I tried the window to that room but it was locked from the inside and the room was empty. I had nothing to break the glass with, so continued running.

Don't think, I ordered myself. Don't think about how the back entrance door leads into the main hallway, and you'll have at least ten feet to run in the hallway before you get to the gym door. Don't think about Keith standing in the hallway, aiming a gun, throwing his knife, pushing a button that detonates an explosion...

If I didn't know that Chad was somewhere near Keith right then, by choice, and Mr. Seecord was running down the hallway right then, by choice, I would have dropped to the ground outside the back entrance and curled into a ball and let out every scream I'd held in since birth. But there was no time for me to feel, or process, or put things in order. There was only time to do what was right.

I yanked open the door and raced inside. The hallway looked empty at first. As I ran I saw two figures at the other end, bordered in sunlight coming through the entrance doors.

They stood a few feet apart, and had I not known, I would have assumed they were two guys having a casual conversation. Where was Mr. Seecord?

Keith's back was to me and I sent up a prayer of thanks to Tasha's God, and added a cry for help as Keith's head turned. I spotted Mr. Seecord, flattened against a door between two sets of lockers. He had just put his head out to see Chad and Keith. I had just put my hand on the gym door handle.

Chad saw us and shouted something, drawing Keith's attention back to him. Keith yelled and took a step forward. Chad's arms went out and up in the universal sign for surrender.

I desperately wanted to stay, to wait and make sure Chad wouldn't get hurt. Mr. Seecord looked back and saw me. He pointed emphatically toward the gym door. I got the message, pulled the door open, and slipped inside, then ran toward the intercom positioned on the other side of the gym. So many kids had used the intercom for stupid pranks, the school had installed a glass enclosure around it with a lock. I pushed Mr. Seecord's key in and turned it. The keychain dangled and I saw children in his photo. Were they his? I never thought to ask if he had a family. Would he make it home to them tonight?

With a clink, the glass shifted away and I pushed the protruding red button. "Attention, students," I said, praying my voice sounded calm enough that people would know this wasn't a prank, but urgent enough that they'd believe me and get moving. I dared not guess what Keith would do at my words. "Red alert. This is an emergency. All students leave the school building through your classroom windows. Do not—I repeat, DO NOT—go into the hallway." I took a deep breath and waited for my heart to slow, but it didn't. "Go out the windows and run toward the trees across the field. Get away from the school building." Tears stung the back of my eyes.

Would Keith push a button and blow up the building before any of us could get out? "This is not a drill and not a joke. If you hear shooting, drop to the ground, or if you are still close to the building, run in a zigzag pattern. Please go. Go now!"

Everyone in the school would know that message came either from the principal's office near the front of the building, or from the gym. Keith would know. I had to get out before he came after me.

The doors leading from the gym outside were padlocked during the day. I ran to them just in case today was an exception and someone had unlocked them, but they held fast. I looked out the small square windows centered on the doors and saw students flooding out onto the field. Teachers directed them toward the trees, looking back with fear on their faces toward the school. Perhaps the threat about Keith's bomb had spread more than Mr. Seecord thought. Or perhaps after last year, no one wanted to risk hesitating if there was even a chance my announcement was true.

With a quick, darting glance, I took stock of the gym to see if there was a safe place I could hide. Mr. Seecord said he thought the bomb threat was a bluff. Waiting here felt a much safer option than appearing in that hallway again after giving that message. I pictured Keith standing just outside the door and wrapped my arms around myself.

I had decided to try squeezing under a set of stairs behind some boxes when I heard the volley of shots. I raced to the door and heard another single shot and a shout. Too afraid to open the door, I stood clinging to the handle, sobbing.

Mr. Seecord's recognizable yell gave me hope. With my own cry of relief, I thrust open the door and rushed into the hallway. The principal and several arriving teachers, with Mr. Seecord, created a semi-circle over the two bodies on the floor near the entrance.

A long gun lay next to Keith's body and a small gun was in his hand. Blood spread in a pool beneath his head. There was no question he was dead.

I ran, ignoring the teachers, bypassing Mr. Seecord. Why weren't they helping Chad? Why were they just leaving him in that terrible position on the floor?

"Chad!" I dropped to my knees and shouted at him to get up. I vaguely felt hands on my arms, murmurs of teachers trying to get me to back away. I shoved them off and grabbed the collar of Chad's shirt. "Get up!" I yelled. "You saved them. You saved the school. You have to get up so I can tell you how proud I am of you." Tears ran down my face and dropped onto his chest. I looked down and saw that my white top was red. Covered in my best friend's blood.

Every scream I had ever restrained congealed within me, and burst from my soul in one despairing wail that would not stop.

Random Fact: After sustaining trauma to the brain, some people develop "alien hand syndrome," a condition where the victim can feel sensation in the hand, but has no control over movement and does not sense the hand as a part of the body, as if it belonged to an alien being.

Sometimes even the body cannot accept reality.

CHAPTER FORTY-FIVE

I spent two full days in the bathtub. I rocked back and forth in my dark concrete cell, the shower curtain closed, the blinds shut tight, my windowsill empty. I didn't care if it was immature; I wanted to be a child again. I didn't care if it was an avoidance tactic; I wanted to avoid everything, the whole world, myself. Mom came up several times but each time I asked her to leave and out of respect or understanding, she did. It wasn't always silent. I heard people come and go downstairs, murmurs of sympathy and questions of concern. Cameron came that second morning, but I had retreated into the world of my childhood and there was no place for him there. I relived my memories, from Chad's beaming smile in kindergarten when I finally let him move that red car without panicking, to his grin just days ago as we joked about finding a bomb.

The bomb was real. Alecia sat outside my bathroom door the second evening and told me the police found it behind a secret metal panel Keith had built into his locker. That's why the metal detector hadn't been able to locate it. The kid who'd gotten Keith's old locker was a freshman, so didn't notice the space in his locker was smaller than the others.

I didn't care. I wanted to scream at her to leave, but she was sobbing about how Dan had spent the past two days shooting free throws on his back yard goal and couldn't talk about it and she had to talk to someone. I couldn't send her away, but I did plug my ears. I was unable to let my own chasm of grief out, not even in tears, and her loud crying made me want to scratch my hands down my face until it bled. Eventually I heard Mom's voice outside the door. She spoke softly to Alecia, suggested she go home and get some rest. School would be opening again the following day.

Alecia's steps faded away and Mom's voice came through the door. "Victoria." It was full of concern and pity, but not the terrible kind. "I don't expect you to go to school tomorrow," she said gently, "but I do think it would be good if you moved at least into your bedroom. Ate something. Got some sleep."

In the silence, while I knew she waited, I tried to make my mouth speak. The bathtub was hard. My bones hurt and I desperately needed rest, but I couldn't get up. If I moved, that would be choosing to go on living, to move forward, to continue on. I had to stay in this dark, awful nothingness because anything else meant accepting Chad was gone.

Eventually, she moved away from the door and I spent the night detached from my surroundings and the reality outside of them. When the morning light filtered through the cracks in the blinds, forcing me to acknowledge another day no matter how tightly I tried to shut out the sunshine, I heard a new, heavier set of footsteps approach the door. Cameron's voice, raw and wounded, came to me and brought pain with it. "Victoria...please...your parents are worried sick about you. Your friends don't know what to do, and I..." I heard a slight thump as he leaned against the door. "I need you. I'm selfish to say it. I know I should be here in case you need me, and that's why I came the first time. You were the first person I thought of when I heard..." Was he crying? "But I'm not here for you now. He killed my baby brother, and I can't bear it. He shot my brother, Vicky. Not just once. He pumped him through with bullets. How do I live with that? How do I go on when—"

He broke down. I heard his weight fall against the wall outside the door and slide down. I pictured him sitting on the carpet, his head in his hands, and I could not stay in my tub and reject his pain. Very slowly, for each move hurt after being curled up so long, I pulled on a towel rack and stood. I used the toilet and the sink to balance while life came back into my legs and into my consciousness. Both hurt with sharp pricks and I had to wait, head down, hands gripping for support, until the pain subsided enough to move. The sound outside the door had stopped and I wondered if he had gone.

I stepped to the door and touched the knob. I wasn't ready, not to face Cameron or life or reality or anything. But I didn't think I ever would be. I turned the doorknob and pulled the door inward. Cameron sat as I'd imagined him, his head in his hands, a picture of the despair I felt.

Telling myself to have Chad's courage, I slid to sit beside his brother, the one still living, the one hurting, and I put my arms around him. He turned into me and buried his head against my shoulder and cried. I sat, my eyes closed, my heart closed, until it was impossible to keep Cameron's grief and all the reasons for it from coming in, like bullets that let gaping holes in their wake.

I put my head down against his and we wept together for his brother and my best friend.

Random Fact: A duck's quack doesn't echo anywhere, and no one knows why.

Some say that's a myth, but it doesn't matter. There are many things we cannot explain or understand, and we don't know why.

CHAPTER FORTY-SIX

After Cameron left on Thursday, I went to bed and slept twelve hours. I woke up at eight p.m. and spent the night staring into the darkness and thinking about life and death. And Chad.

Time passes slowly when you are grieving. Mom stayed home from work Friday. She came upstairs with food and I ate for her sake. When Dad got home, he came up with an old photo album from when Chad and I were kids, and he talked as I lay there about his memories of those times. Alex came up after supper and sat with me for awhile, eating cookies, offering the plate to me on occasion.

"The kids in my school said Keith was going to blow up your school. Is that true?" He looked at me all guilty. "Mom said I shouldn't ask you any questions. Should I not ask you any questions?"

His mention of Keith pierced through my numbness like a sharpened knife, but I couldn't hope to stay numb forever. "It's okay," I said. "Yes, he—" I couldn't say his name. "—he wanted to set off his bomb in my school."

"And kill everybody?"

"A lot of people."

Alex stopped eating and looked at me. "So Chad saved your life."

I put my hands over my eyes. I nodded.

"Your friend Shane came to visit a day or two ago." I wasn't looking at Alex anymore, but I could hear him chewing. "He said that Chad kept Keith talking so he wouldn't go on a shooting spree, and Keith bragged about hiding the bomb in the locker. And when Keith got out the thingy to push the button and blow everybody up, Chad and Mr. Seecord both ran and tackled him and stopped him."

My mind saw them, standing down the hallway, Chad's arms out as he called Keith's name to divert his attention from me. Protecting me. I felt his kiss on my forehead and pressed my palms hard against my eyelids.

"Mr. Seecord grabbed him from behind and knocked away the bomb remote, but Keith jerked his gun up with his other hand and fired a bunch of bullets right as Chad pushed him to the ground. When Keith saw that he'd killed Chad, and Mr. Seecord was about to pin him to the ground, he got out his pistol and—"

"No more," I said. "Don't say anymore, Alex, please." I saw the blood. On Chad. On me as I begged him to open his eyes and be alive.

"Do you think he knew?" Alex asked. "Chad. Do you think he knew that he would die?"

"I think he knew he might."

"But he did it anyway." Alex's voice held awe. "Wow. He was a real hero."

I nodded as Alex picked up his plate and left the room. "Yes, he was."

Chad's funeral was scheduled for Saturday afternoon. I hadn't seen anyone but my family and Cameron since Monday. Chad would have been the one to go visit friends and make sure everyone was okay. He'd help them overcome. But I wasn't Chad, and he wasn't around to make me better than I was.

I walked into the church, his church, where the funeral would be held, and stopped short seeing the casket. It was open. Why had they left it open?

I didn't want to move closer but part of me had to. Chad was in there. Not really him anymore, but his body. "I can't bear to see him when he isn't really there," I whispered to Mom beside me in the aisle, "but I can't bear not to."

"You need to go, Victoria," she said. Her hand gripped mine. "You need to say goodbye. And you need to have a final memory of him that is not...violent."

Bloody, she meant. Bullet ridden. Connected to a kid who let drugs and hate destroy himself and an amazing person.

I moved forward down the aisle. Something in me recognized that Tasha sat crying on the front row, and I told myself to sit beside her later and comfort her if I could, but my focus remained on Chad's face, now visible from where I stood, his hair still short and fuzzy around his head. It would never grow out now.

Whoever had—I shuddered—prepared him, had done so thoughtfully. His body, from the shoulders down to his feet, was covered with cards and letters and notes, some I recognized from the hospital.

None of the gunshots had hit him from the chest up, so his face looked fine...healthy...normal. Asleep. I got close enough to grip the side of the casket with one hand, and I spoke to my friend. "Goodbye, Chad," I whispered. "I'm very, very mad at you for leaving." I reached in and touched where his heart used to beat. His strong heart that had conquered cancer. "I'll miss you so much."

His face looked so peaceful, I wanted to remain a little longer, but people were behind me waiting for their time to say goodbye. I turned to go and that's when I saw it. Chad's duck. Someone had tucked it into his casket with him.

Random Fact: At only 6-13 weeks of development, the whorls of what will be fingerprints, one of the most unique human traits, have already developed in fetuses. Those fingerprints will not change throughout the person's life and will be one of the last things to disappear after death.

From the beginning to the end, there is no one like you in the world, and will never be again.

CHAPTER FORTY-SEVEN

Chad's parents had asked me to say something, and I dreaded it like I'd never dreaded anything in my life. They went first, after the pastor, but Mrs. Carlson broke down and couldn't finish. Cameron spoke next, and his funny stories about when Chad was a kid had us laughing through our tears. Tasha had been given the option to speak, but she said she couldn't set her feelings for Chad out on display.

I was next. Knowing that my mind would shut down the moment I stood in front of a crowd of people, with Chad's casket below me, his face white and still, I had written out what I wanted to say. The paper in my hand came from that pink notebook Chad refused to have his facts written in. Aside from this torn-out page, the notebook was still blank and would remain so forever. I unfolded the paper to set it on the podium, and made my voice monotone as I read so I could get through the words.

"Chad wrote an essay on what was worth living and dying for. In it, he said the chance to really live was a gift, and he refused to waste it. As he read that, we all thought of his cancer, and how he fought death so he could live. None of us knew that the next day he would give up his life for us." I paused, took in a breath, and kept going without looking up, unable to bear seeing Tasha or Alecia or Dan right then. "A bomb was placed in the center of our school building. Had it gone off between classes with kids all over the hallway, many, many of us would have died. Chad's courage saved my life. He gave all of us the chance to really live, and now it is my turn to say I refuse to waste that gift." Emotion was creeping in. I cleared my throat and tried not to think about the words I was saying. I needed to say them, for Chad, and if I started crying I'd never get them out. "Pretty much every fear I've ever faced was because of Chad. He's been my best friend for as long as I can remember and there will be a big, big hole—" I cleared my throat again and sniffed. "He said he would make choices that matter, and I choose that too. I'm going to try new things, even if I'm scared. I'm going to love people better, and try to protect myself less, to make the right choice instead of the safe one. I'm going to read Chad's Bible, cover to cover just like he did, and search for the answers he found that gave him such wisdom and hope."

My paper speech was done. I avoided looking at the people filling the auditorium and instead let my gaze fall on the yellow duck tucked into Chad's casket. "If what Chad discovered and put his faith in is true, then he's in heaven right now, far away from cancer and pain and darkness and fear, and for that, I am happy for him. I'm going to find out for myself if it's true." I looked upward. "I don't know how it works in heaven, but if you can see me right now...if you can hear me, Chad..." I had to blink and two tears dropped from my eyes and ran down the sides of my upturned face. "Thank you."

We got to the cemetery just as the first rays of dusk fell over the graves. The pond turned fiery orange in the fading sunlight and the ducks returned to their safe havens for the night. I turned away when they closed Chad's casket. He wasn't there anyway. They lowered his body into the ground and people did ceremonious rituals in exchange for a hollow sort of comfort. Then they lined up and hugged Mr. & Mrs. Carlson and Tasha, who stood weeping at their side. I wandered away, not wanting to be hugged or cried over, or told time would make things better or the hundred other things people say at funerals that they shouldn't.

Cameron found me later, my knees up to my chest, my arms wrapped around them, sitting on the ground by the pond where I'd sat so many times with the four dorks and now sat alone. I felt his presence before I actually saw him. He came from the side, slowly, like he hesitated to interrupt my solitude. "You can sit down if you want," I said.

"I need to tell you something." He remained standing, a few feet to my left and back a little. "From Chad."

I glanced over my shoulder. He had Chad's bag in his hands. I looked back out over the water. "Okay."

"It doesn't make any sense to me, but he said you'd understand." Cameron set the bag on the ground and opened it. "He asked me to do this for him if he died. That was back when he was in ICU with the cancer, but I know he'd still want me..." Cameron left the sentence unfinished. Yes, whether from cancer or a killer, death was death, and it had taken away my friend. I would want whatever message Chad had for me.

"First, he said to give you this."

I turned and the tears came afresh. Cameron held out a plastic yellow rubber ducky. Mine. I had assumed it sat alone on Chad's windowsill now that Chad's was buried with him. I reached out and took the duck from Cameron's hand and turned it over to see my name, scrawled in fat, childish letters, on the bottom.

"Next I'm supposed to do this." He walked up to the edge of the pond and turned Chad's bag over. Rubber duckies of all shapes and sizes fell out to land on the water, at least forty or fifty of them. Cameron dropped the bag on the ground and sat beside me. We watched the ducks bob in the water and then float. Some banged into each other. Others drifted off by themselves.

"You're supposed to put yours in," Cameron said. "Chad said to tell you, 'It's okay. You can go now.'"

I put my head down on my knees, my duck tight in my hand. Long minutes passed while I stayed still and thought through all it would mean to let my duck go, the duck I'd given to Chad, out into the pond with all the others, free to find a cluster of other ducks or float off alone, while Chad's was now in the ground.

"Like I said, I don't get it," Cameron said, "so it's okay with me if you want to keep your duck. I know it's special to you." He stood. "What you said at the funeral was really beautiful. Did you mean it?"

I wiped my eyes and looked up at him. "Mean it?"

"That you were going to choose to really live." He turned to look across the cemetery, across a hill full of graves to where Chad's fresh plot stood, covered in flowers, the area shaded by a portable overhang that someone would remove before nightfall. "I kind of want to just go home and sit in the dark and be sad." Cameron's voice was soft, like the breeze that brushed across my skin. He ran his hand over the side of his head and the hair above his right ear stuck out. "But what you said meant something. Chad wouldn't want that. He'd want us to live. So how about we start right now?" He reached out a hand to me. "Would you come with me to...anywhere? We can get something to eat and talk about the great things we remember about Chad. I want to talk about him, about the good things. Will you come with me, Victoria?"

I looked at his hand, reaching out for mine, and then I looked at my duck. Could I? Could I choose to really live when I didn't want to? To move forward? To continue on and find goodness and hope instead of hiding in the dark? It would not be a safe choice. But it might be the right one.

Standing, I leaned forward and set my duck in the water. It floated across the ripples and merged into the crowd of ducks, rubbing up against them, turning and being carried first one way, then another. "We can't just leave the ducks in the pond," I said. "It's probably illegal."

"We'll come back for them later, I promise."

Cameron still held out his hand in invitation. With one last glance at the pond—at my duck floating with all the others—I put my hand across the space between us and placed it in his. With my other hand I reached up to smooth the hair above his ear. I looked at Cameron Carlson and said, "Yes. It's okay. I can go now."

And I did. To life. To a future and a hope.

kimberly rae

Greater love
has no one
than this,
than to lay down
one's life
for his friends.

-Jesus
John 15:13

kimberly rae

A place to write your own thoughts
on What's Worth Living and Dying For:

And you will seek Me
and find Me,
when you search for Me
with all your heart.

-God

Jeremiah 29:13

Where to look in the Bible for answers
on What's Worth Living and Dying For:

John 14:1-6
Matthew 16:25-26
John 15:11-13
Matthew 6:19-20
Matthew 6:25-34
Ephesians 2:10
2 Corinthians 5:17
Psalm 16:11
Psalm 143:8

What God thinks about You:
Jeremiah 31:3
Psalm 139
John 3:16

kimberly rae

More Random Facts, for anyone who wants to start their own notebook.

Note: Most of my random facts came from the internet, and as we all know, not everything on the internet is true, so if a fact is super important to you for some reason, you should probably check it out for sure before, say, quoting it at your high school graduation or somebody's wedding.

-The silkworm consumes 86,000 times its own weight in 56 days.

-In the state of Queensland, Australia, it is still constitutional law that all pubs must have a railing outside for patrons to tie up their horse.

-The bloodhound is the only animal whose evidence is admissible in court.

-The elephant is the only mammal that can't jump.

-In New York State, it is still illegal to shoot a rabbit from a moving trolley car.

-Some hospitals keep a supply of beer for alcoholics in case they go through withdrawal, which can be fatal. Some hospitals even have beer cans with prescription labels.

-Six billion steps of DNA are contained in a single cell.

-John Kellogg invented corn flakes for a patient with bad teeth.

-Every citizen of Kentucky is required by law to take a bath at least once a year.

-More people in the world have mobile phones than toilets.

-American car horns beep the tone F.

-After eating too much, your hearing is less sharp.

-Google was originally called Backrub.

-Beer is made by fermentation caused by bacteria feeding on yeast cells and then defecating. In other words, it's a nice tall glass of bacteria doo-doo.

-Rubber bands last longer when refrigerated.

-China has treatment camps for internet addicts.

-Everyone has a unique smell, except for identical twins.

-The first web camera was created in Cambridge to check the status of a coffee pot.

-Nigeria makes more movies every year than the US.

-High school students spend an average of six times as many hours on the internet than they do on homework.

-You can't plow a cotton field with an elephant in North Carolina.

-It is against the law to whale hunt in Oklahoma.
(Think about it...)

abnormal results

kimberly rae

OTHER BOOKS BY KIMBERLY RAE

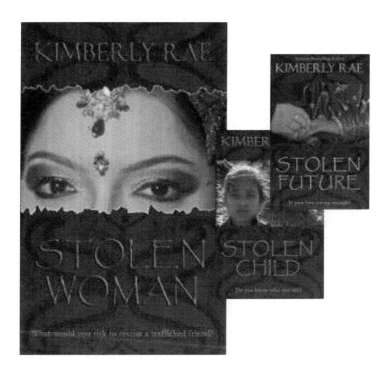

Human Trafficking...Asha knew nothing about it before meeting 16-year-old Rani, stolen from her home and forced into prostitution in Kolkata, India. Asha must help this girl escape, but Mark, a third-generation missionary, keeps warning her away from the red-light district and its workers. Will she ever discover why? And will they ever stop their intense arguments long enough to admit their even more intense feelings for one another? When Asha sneaks out one last time in a desperate attempt to rescue her friend, someone follows her through the night. Is freedom possible? Or will she, too, become one of the stolen?

Jasmina, a young girl in India, and her brother, Samir are sold by their father to a man promising them an education and good jobs.

They soon discover the man is providing an education, not in a school, but as a slave in his sweatshop garment factory. While Samir quickly submits to his new life of misery, Jasmina never stops planning an escape.

She comes to realize that escape doesn't always mean freedom.

FIND THESE AND OTHER BOOKS AT

www.kimberlyrae.com

kimberly rae

ACKNOWLEDGMENTS

My thanks to Amy Helms Grant for sharing your family's cancer experience with me. May you have grace, courage, and strength as you all continue to fight.

Thanks, Cassie and Aidan, for offering your hands so this book could have an awesome cover. I owe you a duck.

Thank you to Nancy and Zachary for your feedback and enthusiasm for this book.

Thanks to Susan and Patrick King, for your inspiring example of not letting autism define or hinder you.

My appreciation to the Facebook friends and fans who give feedback and help me know what readers like best. I love sharing my author adventures with you.

Thanks, as always, to Brian for loving me enough to listen to me read every single book aloud, even the ones for girls.

Biggest and best thanks go to Jesus, the reason I wanted to write a book that offered not just hope through cancer, but hope through life and death and everything in between.

kimberly

ABOUT THE AUTHOR

Kimberly Rae is abnormal. She talks too much when she gets nervous, and can't stand to have anything touching her neck. She thinks lima beans taste like paper towels, and, ironically, finds teenagers totally intimidating.

Award-winning author of 20 books, Rae has been published over 300 times and has work in 5 languages.

Rae lived in Bangladesh, Uganda, Kosovo and Indonesia. She now writes from her home at the base of the Blue Ridge Mountains in North Carolina, where she lives with her husband and two young children. Her Stolen Series, suspense and romance novels on human trafficking, are all Amazon bestsellers.

Find out more or order autographed books at
www.kimberlyrae.com.

43177303R00127

Made in the USA
Lexington, KY
21 July 2015